Gr

Sheelagh Mawe was b
Hertfordshire, and at
School for Girls. She li\ ... ᴧᴧance for five years
where she was employed as a tour guide for
Champagne Mercier. She then moved to Florida
where she became a tennis enthusiast and worked
for some years managing a tennis club there.
Sheelagh Mawe now lives in Orlando where she has
set up her own gift company together with her two
sons. *Grown Men* is her first novel.

SHEELAGH MAWE

Grown Men

INDIGO

First published in the USA 1997 by Avon Books

First published in Great Britain 1998
by Victor Gollancz

This Indigo edition published 1999
Indigo is an imprint of Orion Books Ltd,
Orion House, 5 Upper St Martin's Lane,
London WC2H 9EA

Published by arrangement with William Morrow & Company
Publishers, a division of the Hearst Corporation

Copyright © 1997 by S. M. Mawe

The right of Sheelagh Mawe to be identified as author
of this work has been asserted by her in accordance with
the Copyright, Designs and Patents Act, 1988.

A catalogue record for this book is
available from the British Library.

ISBN 0 575 40143 5

Siddartha, Hermann Hesse, copyright 1951 by New
Directions Publishing Corporation. Reprinted by permission
of New Directions Publishing Corporation.

Printed and bound in Great Britain by
Guernsey Press Co. Ltd, Guernsey, Channel Isles

All rights reserved. No part of this publication may be
reproduced or transmitted in any form or by any means,
electronic or mechanical including photocopying,
recording or any information storage or retrieval system,
without prior permission in writing from the publishers.

This book is sold subject to the condition that it shall not,
by way of trade or otherwise, be lent, resold, hired out, or
otherwise circulated without the publisher's prior consent
in any form of binding or cover other than that in which it
is published and without a similar condition including this
condition being imposed on the subsequent purchaser.

For Mike, Amanda, and Andrew

The true profession of man is his
journey to himself . . .

Herman Hesse, *Siddhartha*

ONE

Jack . . . I hear the blast of his car horn, see his reflection in my rearview mirror, just as I come off the Interstate and turn east towards the club, and though I wave a hand out my sunroof, smile at his reflection, behind my sunglasses I'm thinking, Shit . . .

I planned on getting there way ahead of him. I wanted to see who was playing where . . . say my hellos . . . sign us up a court someplace out in the nether regions, if possible, where his noisy shouts and flashy play wouldn't attract the wrong kind of attention. And now I'm not going to have time for any of it.

Don't get me wrong. Jack's OK. The kind of guy men like and women go crazy over. The kind you'd call a charmer if your taste runs to diamonds in the rough. But he can be brash. Crude too. And having him playing on the next court isn't everyone's idea of a good morning's tennis. Besides, next to Jack's flamboyance, the rest of us look dull, colorless . . . And that's not a way I like to look.

I've known Jack a long time. So long I can't remember a time I didn't know him. He was part of the neighborhood I grew up in where his stocky frame and jeering, laughing face were as familiar and ever present as the houses we lived in, the streets we played on. He was part of my school days too, grade school through high, and as best I can remember, I spent them all in a state of shocked admiration at the way he handled teachers, and green-eyed with envy over his swaggering bravado around girls. Girls who even at that age swarmed him in giggling, adoring groups.

My parents, particularly my mother, thought him the devil incarnate, thought the whole teeming family a plague to the neighborhood. 'You stay away from that bunch, Austin Sinclair,' she warned – she always called me by my full name, my mother – 'They're wild. Undisciplined. Bad examples.'

I stayed away. Not because of what she said, but because even that young I felt plain and slow-witted next to him. I couldn't think of quick, funny things to say off the top of my head as he could and I didn't have his bold self-confidence or dark good looks. I was tall and pale-skinned, and my hair, which barely saw me through my twenties, was nondescript. I blushed easily, and though my head teemed with carefully thought-out witticisms, they never came out the way I rehearsed them and always a beat too late, so I stayed away by choice.

Despite our proximity then, I could have grown up not knowing him at all except one summer – the summer we were ten – a tennis craze swept our neighborhood with all the ferocity of a prairie fire, and when it burned itself out it left behind two permanent casualties, Jack and me. We were hooked and, because we only had each other, became, for a few years anyway, inseparable.

I tilt my head sideways for another look at him in the mirror and wonder, as I've wondered a million times, if he's still the player he was back then, back in the days when beating each other and getting ranked was all that mattered to either of us, and every point was played as though the electric chair were the booby prize.

I don't like being around people who live their lives looking back over their shoulders at the good old days, but dammit, those were good days. Amazing days really, when I think about them. A time when I had only one thing on my mind and all the freedom and energy in the world to pursue it.

Of course, I didn't appreciate them. When I was living them I thought the good old days were yet to come; thought they'd arrive when I was through with school and making money, money being the antidote to all my lacks as I saw them. Money would buy me armloads of racquets and new sneakers before I needed them, not after the soles of my feet were blistering on the court. And money would buy me tennis clothes that both fit and matched, and new balls at least once a week. And I thought if I had all that, I would be happy.

I catch myself making a sound that's somewhere between a laugh and a groan thinking of all the racquets and clothes and sneakers; the houses, the cars, and the you-name-its I've gone through over the years. And then damned if I'm not hearing the words – words that seem to be going off like a gong in my head all the time lately – coming out of my mouth in a pitiful kind of bleat. 'What happened?' they sigh, and Jesus but will you listen to me! I straighten up quick behind the wheel and check the rearview. I know Jack can't hear me. Can't see my lips moving. If they moved. But what's with me anyway?

What happened is I found out otherwise, that's all. I grew up, just like everybody else, and discovered that life isn't as simple as I thought it was going to be. No big drama. Nothing to groan about. Especially not now, thirty years after the fact.

Anyway, along with the tennis, because of the tennis, Jack and I shared a dream, and the dream was to take our tennis all the way to the top, to travel the world with our racquets like Gonzalez and Segura. Well . . . kids have their dreams, and we were the two top-ranked Juniors in the state vying for the number one slot every time the rankings came out, so what was to stop us?

My mother, down on her hands and knees scrubbing the kitchen floor when I told her my plans, stopped me. Pulling herself upright with the help of a kitchen chair, she advanced to where I stood barefoot at the edge of the wet, clean-scrubbed area. 'Austin Sinclair,' she said softly, her eyes holding mine fast, 'was raised to WORK.'

She held my gaze until all the rebellion, all the arguments, died unspoken on my lips and then, satisfied she was understood, returned heavily to her unceasing battle with dirt.

I don't know what Jack's family told him. Don't know if he even discussed his future with them, but deflated by my mother's words our competition lost some of its edge for me, and goaded by the ever-quickening drumbeat, 'College. Work. College. Work,' coming at me from both parents, I started hitting the books in earnest.

Strange the way kids in those days obeyed their parents. Or is what's strange the way they disobey them now? Tell one of my kids they can't do something, go someplace, and they say, 'Oh . . . OK,' and then go right ahead and do it anyway, as though what I just told them was meant for ears other than their own.

In my youth I believed all adults infallible. I thought my destiny carved in stone, and not knowing I had choices, I did as I was told. As in my early years, I had been a dutiful, obedient child, so, as the son of first-generation Americans whose dream for their children included college educations and white-collar jobs, I willingly fleshed out Stage Two of the master plan handed to me. I went away up to the state university and worked my way through.

College was tougher for me than most. An endless daily struggle to keep up with grades and assignments and work. A nonstop, no-win battle against worry and fear and dread. I see now I was no more college material than I was the man in the moon, but I didn't know it at the time. At the time I just thought I was stupid. And so I struggled through and got my degree and came away feeling no more prepared to take on the world than when I started except for one thing: I knew for certain what I'd been vaguely aware of all along. I knew that persistence paid.

Stage Three of my prearranged destiny had to do with marrying a good stable girl and raising good healthy children. And Stage Four was all about taking care of self-sacrificing parents in their old age. I did those too.

Anyway, back to Jack and tennis. In fairness, our leaving it wasn't all my mother's doing. Part of it was we were growing up, widening our interests. And most of that interest centered on the girls that came to watch us play. Not nuisance, giggling girls anymore but soft pretty ones with promises in their smiling eyes and secrets under their clothes. They were there for Jack, and I knew it. That didn't stop me from looking, though. And then, when I was a senior, there came a girl amazingly oblivious to Jack's charms. Her name was Ellen and she came for me . . .

Slowly then, so slowly I don't remember now where or when we played our last match nor even who won, the tennis slipped away, and Jack and I, our only mutual interest gone, drifted apart.

As I said, I went away to school. And Jack? Well, the day after graduation – high school graduation, that is – old Jack up and married the most beautiful girl in town. That's not quite right. I married the most beautiful girl in town. I married Ellen, the Homecoming Queen. But not until I'd sweated out those college years and not because I had to. Not like Jack.

My mother, habitually hard-pressed for family news in her weekly letters ('Your father, your sister, and I are well . . . '), nevertheless found plenty to say about Jack. It seemed to me she gloried in the misfortunes that plagued him until I realized she was holding him up to me as the bad example she'd always said he was. Saying in so many words, 'See! What did I tell you? Didn't I always say they were a shiftless bunch? And didn't I tell you you'd thank me one day? That boy doesn't know the meaning of self-discipline. Hard work.'

For Jack, it seemed, was drifting in and out of piddling

jobs at the rate of one a week. Jack and his bride and his baby, a son, couldn't pay the rent. They moved in with his family. They moved back out. Jack owed everybody. Jack got fired again. Jack's wife left him. She came back. She was gone again.

Then in my junior year the tone of the letters changed. There was a hint of surprise in the crowded pages. Jack had gone to work for one of the local boat manufacturers. Jack had talked his way into the selling end of it. Jack was doing well. Jack, for God's sake, was a YACHT SALESMAN!

As Jack turned his life around, my mother's letters got close to hysterical. 'He's bought himself a house!' one of them gasped. 'He's driving a Cadillac!' exclaimed another. When he bought his parents a new car, the first they ever owned, the tone of the letters grew peevish. My mother was floundering, and in between the lines I read what I wondered myself: How could a person flout all the rules and in a few years' time earn and spend more than my parents had accumulated in a lifetime? What had happened to HARD WORK and SELF-DENIAL and COLLEGE DEGREES? And what about STAYING AWAY FROM THE GIRLS and SAVING FOR THE FUTURE? Old Jack hadn't bought any of it and where was he? A damn sight further along than me, that's where.

It really bugged me, summers I was home, seeing him ride around town in that big yellow Eldorado he bought himself, his gorgeous wife mashed up so tight against his side, the wonder was he could steer at all.

Shit, no wonder I burned. All I had was a worn-out bicycle, a summer job pumping gas, and my girl, my Queen, saying, 'I'd like to, honey, honest I would . . . but . . . what if I got pregnant? I mean . . . we have to get ahead first, right?'

I'd have liked, those times I was home, to talk to Jack, find out how in hell he'd gone so far so fast. Ask him how he got to the top without climbing the stairs. I mean, Jesus, what were the magic words? But I never did. Too proud, I guess. Hell, he was the blue-eyed wonder boy of the town then, a man in every sense of the word, and I was still a school kid sweating exams and working shit jobs and worrying just how far ahead I was going to have to go to get Ellen in bed with me. Damn, but I waited a long time for that woman. A long, long time.

Took me five years of eighteen-hour days to get my degree, the extra year because I had to drop out altogether to scrape up enough cash to finish, then two more after that to work up from an entry-level position in a local bank to Branch Manager. And one more after that before Ellen considered me far enough ahead to give up her virginity two nights after the day I married her.

Ellen never liked Jack, and that still surprises me given the way every other female in town throws herself at him. But by the time we were married, Jack and I had long since moved out of each other's orbits anyway.

Not that I haven't seen him around, because I have. And this being the town it is, what I haven't seen, I've heard. But I've never done anything about staying in touch on a personal level. For one thing, my feelings towards him have always been so ambivalent, such an uneasy mix of admiration and disapproval, it was easier to follow Ellen's lead and

16

just stay away. And for another, my bride wasn't going to be happy until she reigned over the town's social scene the way she'd reigned over the school scene, and to please her, though I had my hands full earning the kind of living she expected, I jockeyed my way into every club and onto the boards of every organization the town had to offer. All places and situations Jack avoided like the plague.

For years then, a nod or a wave of the hand as we pass has been about the extent of our communication. Or they were until I ran into him again one day earlier this week . . .

That day, feeling impatient, bored, as though I ought to be somewhere else but not knowing where, I was looking around a crowded noontime restaurant when I ought to have been giving my full attention to the guy I was with – a guy who was about to swing a deal that would put a large chunk of money in my bank – when Jack walked in.

Of course, he wasn't alone. You never see Jack alone. He was at the center of a noisy group, all of them falling over themselves laughing at some story he was telling. And watching, seeing them all so damn carefree, I suddenly felt such an unexpected surge of regret, such nostalgia for times gone by, that, surprising myself as much as my client, who I left in startled midsentence, I found myself on my feet, hurrying across the room to grab him by the elbow before he could sit down.

He didn't act surprised. Not nearly as surprised as I would have if he'd come barreling across a room at me after so many years.

'How's it going?' I asked, reaching for his hand and shaking it.

'S'going great,' he said. 'How about yourself?'

'Couldn't be better. Say . . . you playing any these days?'

'Some . . . '

'Want to hit a few sometime? Soon?'

He grinned, his teeth startling white in his sunburned, bearded face.

'Anytime,' he said.

'How about Saturday?'

'Saturday's good with me.'

'Ten o'clock?'

'You got it. Where?'

'My club?'

He nodded, gave me the thumbs-up sign, and turned back to his friends.

Grinning like a fool, feeling like I'd been given an unexpected present, which I had, the pleasure of something to look forward to, I said, 'See you,' and hurried back to my client.

Of course, my mood hadn't lasted, and soon I was wondering why in hell I'd let a bleak moment and a childish impulse bring someone back into my life who was probably better off out of it. And I was complaining inwardly because my invitation had implied singles, and singles are something I rarely play in the summertime anymore, particularly not this one when every record for heat here in Florida has been shattered. And on top of all that I had to call and cancel the game I already had lined up Saturday, and felt bad doing it. Hell, I know better. I always have games lined up Saturdays. Sundays too.

Maybe that's why I asked him then. Maybe I was bored

18

beating the same people week after week as I'm bored with everything else going on around me right now. Maybe I needed a challenge.

Anyway, it's too late for reasons now. There he is, sitting on my tail, all flashing teeth and gold chains and shaggy hair, and again I'm thinking, Oh, shit . . . !

Naturally he's got the radio of that red convertible kiddie car of his blasting like he's still some kind of demented teenager, which means he's blown every point in play on the courts we're driving between. It follows then that every face on those courts is turned our way, most of them in outrage, and that's what I meant earlier when I said he can attract the wrong kind of attention.

He must be reading my thoughts, sensing my embarrassment, because suddenly the volume of his radio goes up louder still and in my mirror I see his head thrown back in laughter, his shoulders shimmying in time to the music.

And in spite of myself, I'm grinning back. Can't help myself. And grinning, I'm thinking, the hell with a back court. There's no hiding this guy. No burying him. Might as well put him on the stadium court and let him have his head.

TWO

Austin! I laugh out loud seeing him putzing along ahead of me in that immaculate Mercedes of his, twenty minutes ahead of time. I was so sure he'd do that – be early, I mean – I passed on a second cup of coffee just for the pleasure of proving myself right.

Old fart, I think. But I mean it kindly. I've been calling Austin an old fart since we were both eight years old, so if he's old, then I must be too. Getting there anyway. Only I'm not and he is. Austin's one of those guys that are born old, and for all his success, the clout that goes with his name alone, he hasn't grown a day younger since the time his family moved into the old neighborhood what . . . ? Thirty? No. Has to be more like forty years ago. Jesus! Forty years! That's enough to make you old just thinking about it.

I used to bust my ass in those far-off days trying to get Austin to notice me. Maybe I still do. Maybe that's why, seeing him up ahead just now, I had to blast my horn . . . turn up my radio . . . Want to make sure he knows I'm here and pays me some attention.

I guess what he is to me – always has been – is a chal-

20

lenge. It's like I see him as a turtle living closed up tight inside a shell with only its head coming out when it thinks no one's looking. The challenge is to get that head out when I am looking. I know when I'm around him I act different than I do around other people. What I do is, I act outrageous. Can't help myself. It's like it's written somewhere I have to show him he doesn't have to be so frigging careful all the time. Like it's my duty to tell him, 'Hey! Loosen up, boy! See . . . the world doesn't end if you have a little fun. Make a little noise. Drink a little drink. Look at me, for chrissakes. I'm still alive, aren't I?' Some of the worst hangovers I ever had in my life came from trying to educate Austin.

The first time I ever saw him, the day they moved onto our street, I damn near bled to death trying to get his attention.

All morning I'd hung around watching them unload their belongings from a big old truck parked at the curb, thinking how strange they were. Strange to me because they were all tall and blond in a neighborhood where everyone else was short and dark and Italian. Stranger still because they never said a word to one another the whole time they unloaded, and I come from people who never stop talking . . . arguing . . . fighting . . .

'Hey,' I finally said to the boy, watching him back out of the truck carrying one end of a sofa. 'My name's Jack. What's yours?'

'His name is Austin Sinclair,' the mother snapped, setting down her end of the sofa to put herself between him and me, 'and he's got WORK to do.'

Ignoring her, I said, 'How old are you, Austin Sinclair?'

'He's eight,' the mother snarled, 'and I already told you, he's got work to do.'

'Eight?' I breathed, impressed nearly speechless. 'Shit! I'd've said more like fourteen, him being so tall and all . . . '

The mother gasped, shoved Austin back into the van, then whirled on me. 'We don't talk like that around here,' she hissed. 'And I'll thank you to stay away from my boy.'

I took myself off to the middle of the street knowing she'd have to call the cops to get me away from there, and I went through every cuss word I could think of, loud, all the time watching Austin out the sides of my eyes. Nothing. I tried my whistles next. Whistled till I was spitless and sick to death of my own noise, and still nothing. Challenged, I went away home, got my bike, and, one foot on the handlebars, the other on the seat, rode up and down in front of them. In and around them . . . And all I got for my trouble was the mother's voice, pitched low like an attack dog's warning growl, snarling, 'Austin . . . '

I got really mad then and went away and hung myself by my knees from the highest branch of their neighbor's tree. That did it.

'Your nose is bleeding,' Austin said, about the time things were starting to turn black.

'So . . . ?' I said. But I was laughing inside because I'd done what I set out to do. Made him notice me. Talk to me.

'Austin!' the mother roared.

'Get the hell outta my tree, Jack,' the neighbor woman yelled. 'Your blood's making a mess in my yard.'

I was feeling sick and dizzy by then anyway and glad enough to act obedient and come down out of the tree, but I was still intent on finding out more about this kid, so I sat back down in the middle of the street and waited.

After a while the truck, emptied, drove away, and thinking now the work was done, this giant kid they called Austin Sinclair would come out, I waited on. But the house showed as little sign of life as it had all the time it was vacant. Finally, thinking I might be about out of blood, I got on my bike and rode away. And what I was thinking was, old fart . . .

I never did get inside that house of theirs, but I used to wonder, watching Austin come and go from my seat in the school bus, what it could be like inside. Like a church, I finally figured, seeing the mosaic tile his dad set in cement on the front walk. The stone angel staring blank-eyed at a dry birdbath. The unmoving, permanently closed drapes. Exactly like a church. A place of shadows and silence where people would move slow and talk in whispers.

Grass, green and mowed and edged, soon surrounded that house, and I remember seeing that as a novelty. So was their driveway. They edged it in bricks painted white, one leaning just so against the next and kept so clean, I wondered if his mother didn't come out nights and scrub them on hands and knees.

You couldn't tell the other houses had driveways. Couldn't see where the cement ended and the yards began for the accumulated junk of dozens of kids and oil stains and old cars, most often in pieces.

He's not one to move fast, Austin, I'll tell you that. He's

23

given me a nod there, a wave of the hand, but is he going to haul ass and get us out of this endless driveway to the clubhouse we're passing through? No, he is not. He's going to move just as slow and just as careful as he did when we were kids and he took so long thinking about the adventures the rest of us planned that most times we took off without him.

He's forced me to gear all the way down to first here and I'm sitting staring at the back of his head, at the starched white tennis hat he's got set dead straight on top of it, and I'm thinking, what the hell are we here for, Austin? To play tennis or look at the goddam scenery? And suddenly I'm so exasperated, I turn the radio up louder still, until it's nearly blasting me out of my seat, seeing if that won't light a fire under him . . . Forget it. All he's done is close his windows, and I'm left listening to music I can hardly stand wondering why I thought he'd change. Wishing I'd gone for that second cup of coffee. And thinking, if it wasn't for tennis . . .

If it wasn't for tennis, I'd have given up on Austin when I was nine, ten years old. I mean, shit, you go where you're welcome, right?

But one summer day when we were round about that age we got a look at what the game is all about and Austin and I got into it. For a few years I felt like I was up there beside him on that pedestal he lives on.

Lucky for us, it cost the same back then to get into tennis here in Florida as it does now, which is to say, nothing. There're public courts everywhere. They even built one, a slab of cement, in the mangy, treeless park that ran along

24

back of our strip of houses, though until the day I'm telling about, none of us used it to play tennis. Tennis was a sport we didn't know much about. A game we'd only seen played by some of the younger mothers once in a while and one we didn't care to pursue. We thought it was a sissy game. The way they played it, with underhand serves and nervous screams, it was.

Instead, we used the court for basketball and as a race-track for our bikes and roller skates and, more often than any of that, just as a place to hang out.

As I remember that day, that's what we were doing, nothing, when all of a sudden, out of nowhere, a Ferrari sports coupé came steaming in and two guys, strangers to our neighborhood, piled out and helped themselves to our court.

It was the car that grabbed us first. We'd never seen its like before, not outside the covers of a magazine anyway, so it was a while before we stopped admiring it and turned to watch the guys instead.

When we did, we saw a style of play so different from any-thing we'd ever seen before, it was a while before we caught on to what it was they were playing. 'Can it be tennis?' we said, watching, stunned, their great sweeping serves, the net rushing, the overheads, the drop shots.

'Can it be tennis?' we said again, seeing the way they had the ball skimming the net with a thousandth of an inch to spare one minute, then were lobbing it the next, sending it up with so much spin, the ball took on a different shape altogether, like it wasn't a ball at all but a disc instead.

'Holy shit!' we said. 'Let's play tennis!'

Pretty soon every kid on the street was out there watching and a lot of mothers too, babies on their hips.

'I said I'd beat you,' one of the guys said, coming off the court at the end of it. 'And I did. Now, pay up.'

The second guy laughed, pulled out a wallet, and counted out some bills.

The first guy shoved his winnings in his pocket, then held up his racquet to show a dangling, broken string.

'Didn't know I busted my gut on that last game, did you?' he said, and laughing, flipped the thing into the wire trash basket I was leaning up against.

I went rigid with shock, my poor-child's mind not grasping, not comprehending, that there were people in the world who threw things away. Good things. But even as I came to terms with the possibility, my eyes were covering the crowd looking to see who else had seen the unbelievable act. Looking to see what they made of it.

Hardly any had. They were back swarming around the car, waiting to see it come to life. And of those who did, none were close enough to pose a threat. Only Austin.

I saw his eyes light up, his long skinny frame come alert, gather itself . . . He didn't have a prayer. That racquet was in my hands and I was gone, heading for my backyard before he could take step one. I wasn't about to wait around for the guy to change his mind and come back. And I wasn't about to let Austin get his hands on it either. But as I ran, I saw him sinking back, hope dying on his face like someone'd turned out a light. For a second, a split second, because his face had answered my question and told me the guy had honest-to-God thrown the racquet away, I was sorry for

26

him. To make up for it, keep myself straight, I yelled, 'Tough shit, sucker,' and kept on running.

The strangers weren't gone five minutes before our court was crammed with kids wielding ancient racquets and sticks and bats – one girl a shovel – all of us fighting for space, all of us trying to look and play like the guys we'd just seen.

The craze lasted a week, maybe two, and then everyone drifted away until there came a day when there was just Austin and me left, both of us ready to begin.

It came quicker to me than Austin. Most things did. Not that I'm bragging, but Austin couldn't just go out and hit a ball. That would've been too easy. First Austin had to think about it . . . pace the court . . . figure the angles . . . toss a ball around until he understood the spins. Then he had to go to the library and bring home an armful of books and study up on those. And then he had to practice. He wasn't helped any that first summer by his size either. He added another few inches to his already towering frame, and part of his problem was staying out of his own way. But he didn't let that stop him. Nothing ever stopped Austin once he got his mind set on something.

Hardly a morning went by those next few years when you couldn't look up from the old cornflakes and see Austin out the back window slamming a ball against the backboard.

'There's a kid gonna go places,' my dad used to say, stand-ing at my elbow. 'Ain't gonna have no laughs along the way, but he'll get there, see if he don't. The kid's obsessed and that's what it takes. Obsession.'

Austin's obsessed, all right. His obsession with tennis

lasted through high school and then he got obsessed with college. When he got through there, magna . . . whatever the hell it is, he came back, got himself a job at a bank, same one he's running now, and built it into the biggest in the state. Little by little then, in his careful obsessed way, he's gone as far as a man in this town can go. He owns it.

I didn't get to go – to college, I mean – though I could have. Hell, I got better grades standing on my head than old Austin ever did for all his hours of study. But I just couldn't see putting myself through four more years of school. I was a man already. And I had a son to prove it.

College changed Austin, turned him into a snob. A guy who, seeing me coming, all but turned and ran the other way. And that really pissed me off. Especially the first couple years when the world outside of school wasn't exactly living up to my expectations. Not when I was working two, sometimes three, jobs at a time just to cover the rent, it wasn't. Not when I was coming home nights to listen to my wife and my mother and my kid all screaming at me at once, it wasn't.

I laugh now, thinking of the smoke screen I put up to hide behind in those days. The act I put on. The money I threw around. The cars I drove. I was cutting one hell of a figure, all right, but inside there wasn't too much laughing going on. Inside I was a green, shaky kid bluffing my way through the adult world, almost desperate for someone to turn to. There was no talking to my wife. She got hysterical. Nor my dad. He thought I walked on water, and I proved it by buying him a car. The guys I worked with, men twice and three times my age, hated my youthful guts. So that

28

left Austin. Only Austin wasn't talking. Not to me anyway.

Well, I'm glad now he wasn't. Might have taken me longer to learn what I had to learn. I don't know what they teach up there at the university, but where I was I learned what I'd half suspected all along: that life is about playing games. And so I taught myself to play them all. I learned when to listen and when to talk. When to persist and when to turn away. How to hustle and when to close. When to flatter and when to insult. And when I mastered them all, I made it big.

By the time Austin came home for good, I was on a steady roll and ready to get back into tennis, but then I heard he'd gotten himself engaged to Ellen and I made a point of avoiding him the way he avoided me. I mean . . . Ellen?

Ellen is a first-class pain in the ass. One of those golden, small-town princesses raised on bottled water and whole wheat and fresh vegetables to reign over the Senior Prom and later the Junior League and Hospital Auxiliary. The kind that aspire to the right house in the right neighborhood and a maid. The kind that spend their school years mulling over china and silver patterns and playing eenie-meenie-miney-mo with the town's 'promising young men,' figuring which is the sucker most likely to make it all happen for them.

Of our town's crop, Ellen took the prize. A tall, dark beauty back then, she tried her stuff on me a time or two when I was on the Dean's List and looked like college material. A special smile, she had for me then, and a special way of standing close so that as she talked a lock of hair or a breast or thigh brushed up against me.

29

Up until Ellen I'd done all my own chasing, but I wasn't so cool not to have my head turned by so tempting and easy an offer, and after I was sure her tantalizing little movements were no accident, I took her aside and asked her where and when.

There's a lot of Ellens in this world, but she was the first of her kind for me. The one who, while slapping my face and stamping her feet and screaming about the kind of girl she wasn't, showed me the kind she was. A dishonest, conniving cock-tease, is Ellen. Later, when I saw her go to work on Austin and him fall for her line, I was embarrassed for him. Disappointed too. I'd given him credit for more brains.

You can say what you like about my women. God knows I've said plenty myself. But they were honest, all of them, and not the kind to make promises they weren't about to keep.

Ellen's looks are long gone now, buried in the self-satisfied fat of a woman who's achieved her one goal in life, but she hasn't changed any otherwise. I've seen her here and there over the years, and she's still playing the same old games. Acting coy. Butting that massive body of hers against every male that catches her eye. Ellen dances too long and too close with her husband's friends (and the sons of her husband's friends) and nibbles – chews – at their ears and kisses them on the lips, her own parted and moist. And all the while old Austin stands around acting like he doesn't know, hasn't noticed, what's going on, his attitude showing more, I suspect, than he'd like for us to know. That he just doesn't give a damn. So like I said – Ellen?

Anyway, that's enough about her. The point I was coming

to is that Austin and I went our separate ways a long time ago, though he has been on my mind lately as someone I was going to have to get in touch with. And you know how that goes: think about someone long enough and next thing you know they're crossing the street in front of you or calling you up on the phone.

In this instance I'd spent most of a morning picking up the phone and dialing his number only to come unglued and hang up each time his secretary came on the line with her 'Good morning! Mr Sinclair's office!' said ever so brightly.

By noon I was as sick of the sound of her voice as she must have been having a dead phone in her hand and I thought, the hell with it. I took off for lunch hoping I'd run into someone I could coax into buying the sweet little craft I've got sitting in my boatyard. Next thing I know there's old Austin coming right at me saying, 'How're you doing, old guy, old pal?'

Turned out he wanted a game. Do you believe that? With me? A guy he's avoided all his adult life. A guy who makes him wince every time I open my mouth. And at his club yet! The most snobbish 'white and pastel attire only, please' club in the state.

I wanted to ask, why now? What have I got that you want? But like I said, I have wants of my own. I figured I'd find out his end of the deal soon enough. And to tell you the truth, I was tickled. I might not cross a room anymore to say hello to Austin Sinclair, but I'll sure as hell cross a city – maybe even a state – to get him across a net from me again, see what's happened to his game.

I'm watching him up ahead of me now, swinging that precious tank of his in a wide, wide arc so he can back it, ever so carefully, into the last decent shaded space on the lot, and suddenly I have an impulse so strong I can't resist. Accelerating hard, I slam my car headfirst into the space he's aiming for, then I shut my eyes, cover my ears, and pray he's looking over his shoulder.

Of course he is! Didn't I just get through telling you Austin's a careful, thinking man?

THREE

Generally I keep my cussing in my head, where it's safe, but I'm so pissed with Jack right now that, though I know he can't hear me, I call him the son of a bitch he is and, gravel spitting from my rear tires, spin off to the only other available space on the lot. One in full sun next to the fly-infested Dempsey Dumpster.

Ever since this club opened its doors, I've parked in the same space – third slot from the clubhouse on the left. There's a tree there that makes a nice patch of shade, and coming off the court after a long workout, a cool car feels good.

It's not my space per se. That is, it doesn't have my name on it because I voted against reserved parking when we set up the club bylaws, which means anyone can park there if they want to, but nobody does. They know I'm the club founder. They know I'm their number one player. And they know I keep my mouth shut about their finances. So . . . weekend mornings, by what I guess you'd call a gentleman's agreement, it's my space.

And now Jack's sitting in it, grinning like the fool he is.

'Thank you for that,' I say silently, walking towards him.

'Nice of you to remind me this early on what a cheap, unmannerly shit you really are under all that phony charm of yours. You haven't changed at all. What changed were my memories of you. I forgot the rotten side, the way an adult forgets the rainy days of childhood and sees every memory bathed in sunlight.

'But now I'm remembering your other side. The side that took my racquet – the one I mowed lawns a whole summer to buy, the first one I ever had strung in gut – and slung it up in a palm tree where no ladder could reach it, minutes before I was up for the finals of a tournament.

'That racquet stayed up there weeks, rotting and warping before a storm came by to blow what was left of it down. And in the meantime I had to play my match, and all my matches for the next six months, with a borrowed piece of shit from Woolworth's. But I won! A sixteen-year-old clobbering the number one seed in the eighteens. And I won because I was so damn mad, I couldn't think straight. And I'm mad again now. At myself for having you here in the first place. And at you for behaving the way you just did. Disappointed too. I expected better from a grown man. But that's OK. Go on and have your fun. It won't last long. I'm going to beat the shit out of you and get you back in the past where you belong so fast, you won't remember being here. Nobody fucks with my parking space and sits around to laugh about it.'

I'm taking my sweet time walking towards him, stopping every now and then to adjust the racquets in my hand, the carryall I've got slung over my shoulder. I don't believe in hurrying anyway. Never have. To my way of thinking, rushing makes a person look out of control – something I strive never to be – and besides, I need the time to get my anger under wraps where he won't have the satisfaction of seeing he's gotten to me.

Deliberately then as I walk, I make myself relax. I breathe deep, quit scowling down at the ground, and look up to let the Palm Beach opulence I created on these acres here on the West Coast soothe me as it always does. Not bad! Not bad at all, when you consider a few years ago this place was little better than a swamp. A wilderness overgrown with palmettos and stunted oaks trailing poisonous vines and Spanish moss. A morass infested with armadillos and raccoons and rattlers thick as your arm, where the hum of mosquitoes was as loud as the Mormon choir in full voice.

By the time I come alongside of where Jack's lounging against his car, arms folded across his chest, all the anger is gone and I'm wearing a smile that's almost genuine.

'Glad you could make it,' I say, trying not to let the distaste I feel for the clothes he's wearing come through. But I ask you, green nylon running shorts with white stripes down the sides? A faded blue T-shirt? Come on . . .

He's watching me take him in, that cocky smile of his barely restrained, knowing I know he knows the dress code of this club – it was in all the papers – and knowing I know he flouted it on purpose, the way he flouts everything else.

Reminding myself, consoling myself, that in an hour and a half, maybe less, he'll be on his way out of here, I say, 'It's been a long time.'

'Quarter of a century,' he says, eyeing me up and down as

35

though it's me improperly dressed, or else that I'm wearing years instead of clothes. 'More. Only I quit counting.'

'You're looking good,' I lie, seeing the fat settled firm about his throat and paunching over the elasticized waistband of the shorts. Fat that hadn't shown itself under his everyday clothes. Fat that shows me his self-respect is as out-of-shape as the rest of him.

'You too,' he says, and I wonder what he's really thinking. What lies behind the laughter in his eyes.

He's got eyes, Jack, you can't read. Eyes that hide behind drooping lids and thick lashes and always seem to be laughing. Eyes that make you wonder if it's you he's laughing at.

Marveling again at the maudlin impulse that prompted me to invite him here, at a complete loss for words because seeing him like this, away from his entourage, I realize I have no more interest in him than if he were a stranger – a stranger I wouldn't care to know – I head for the Pro Shop, him trailing me juggling a couple of shabby racquets, a towel, and a can of balls. The balls surprise me. Used to be if I didn't provide the balls, we didn't play. Another thing I'd forgotten that always bugged me.

'How's . . . ' I begin and then grope, not remembering, not knowing, his current wife's name or even if he's got a wife at all at the moment. How can I? Jack's gone through so many women, all of them beautiful, no one can keep up with those he marries and those he doesn't. Not even Ellen.

I don't approve of any of it. The divorces . . . the fooling around . . . To me it's sloppy. Untidy. Indecisive. The way I see it, you make a commitment, a vow, then that's it, Charley. You live with your decision. End of story. Not that

36

I haven't been tempted once or twice. But I won't give in to it. It's not my style. I couldn't live with the lies. Besides, I'm too well known. If I started fooling around now, the whole town would know about it before I got my pants zipped up.

'Jennie?' Jack suggests, bringing me back to my question.

'Yes. Jennie. How is she?' And before he can answer I'm putting two and two together, hoping they won't come out to four, and saying, 'You don't mean Jennie Carstairs, do you? I didn't know she . . . I mean, I didn't know . . . That is . . . I didn't realize . . . ' And I'm so taken aback remembering that little girl and the impact she had on all of us the few years she lived here, I can't go on.

Jennie's something special. The kind of woman that can make your day just saying hello. The kind that can turn your knees to water with a smile. And she and Jack . . . ? I remember now seeing her a while back, my eyes coming out of my head at looks that had gone from sensational to downright awesome, and somebody saying she was divorced and here visiting. And I remember thinking that was some kind of asshole she was married to, letting a girl like that get away. But then I hadn't seen her again and I guess I just assumed she'd gone away. But she hadn't! She'd married Jack! And Ellen didn't know . . .

'Yep. That's her,' Jack's saying. 'And she's fine. Said to say hello.' Then he surprises me adding, 'Jennie's for keeps.'

For a moment I feel such contempt for him, such anger, my eyes fill and I'm glad I'm wearing sunglasses. I want to scoff at him. Sneer. I want to say, You? For keeps? You don't know the meaning of the word. And I want to ask, What about all the others? What did you tell them? Before you broke your promises, that is. Your vows . . .

But I say none of it. In a quick sideways glance I see no laughter hidden in his eyes. Only a love so blatant, so naked, I'm shocked and, for a second, so envious, I'm speechless again. He's still getting away with it then! Breaking all the rules and coming away smelling like a rose. Still finding women, sensational women, in spite of the gut and the crude mouth and the poor taste he exhibits in everything he does. Christ! Where's the justice? Isn't a man supposed to reap what he sows?

Finally, when we're inside the Pro Shop waiting to sign up a court, speech returns and, as though there had been no interval, I ask, 'And the kids? How're the kids?'

I don't need to ask. I know how his kids are. I've got two of them working at the bank. His kids are great kids, which is another injustice when you consider how they've been jacked around between wives and ex-wives and grand-mothers and mothers-in-law all their lives.

'Kids are fine,' he says absentmindedly, all his attention taken up by the skintight T-shirt on Cindy, the girl we've got working behind the counter.

'How many do you have now?' I ask, wishing Jennie could get a look at him now.

'Christ. You had to ask. I need to stop and think. You want to know just mine, or his and hers?'

'Uh . . . both, I guess. Altogether.'

'Altogether? OK then. I've got seven.'

'Je-sus!'

'Yeah, right. Je-sus.'

38

'You educating all of them?'

'Trying to,' he says. 'Got two through already. You ought to know, they're working for you. Then one is married, living out of state. And then two of them have dads of their own picking up the tabs, and that leaves two to go.'

He laughs at the expression on my face and slaps me on the shoulder. 'Don't forget I started young.'

'Any living at home with you?'

He shakes his head and his smile disappears. 'Nope. Home's just Jennie and me. How's Ellen?'

I catch myself turning away and stop myself before it's obvious. I'm uncomfortable talking about Ellen, telling people she's fine when if they asked her themselves, they'd hear such a litany of aches and pains, incompetent doctors, pills and diets, uncaring friends and sleepless nights, she'd make me out a liar.

'Ellen's fine,' I say, knowing if she'd quit the booze, she would be.

'And the kids?' Jack is saying, all the while smiling at Cindy, who's smiling back.

'The kids are fine,' I say, glad he isn't paying attention, pushing for details. I'm at the point where I'd just as soon not discuss my kids any more than I want to discuss Ellen. I liked talking about all of them a lot more six or seven years ago when the silver-framed studio pose I have on the edge of my desk didn't tell the lie it tells today. Then they looked like what they were: good-looking, healthy, intelligent kids. A family a man could be proud to be seen with. Now, though they look the same, they're not.

I've got three kids, two sons and a daughter. Kids I'd have

died for when they were small. Kids I'd still die for if anyone said a word against them. But for all that, kids I have a hard time understanding, even liking, anymore. How can I when all the things I took such pride in being able to give them, things I'd wanted them to have because I'd wanted it all so badly myself, aren't where it's at anymore?

'Tennis? You've got to be kidding, man . . . '

'Golf? Forget it . . . '

'A part-time job? What for, Daddy?'

Seems that everything that requires a little time, a little sweat, a little ambition, is too big a hassle. And that's just the small stuff. Come to talk about finishing up their educations, making career decisions, the future. Forget it.

I feel the familiar knot gathering and tightening in my stomach, my mind faltering and growing numb as it always does when it gropes through the chaotic jumble of my shattered illusions. 'What happened?' it moans. And before I can stop myself I'm answering. 'Damned if I know.' And I look up to see Cindy and Jack staring at me.

'He doesn't know,' Jack says, winking at Cindy and tapping his head like I was nuts.

Mystified, she asks, 'What doesn't he know?'

'Which court is open,' I snap back, acting as if it's them being particularly dense. 'What else?'

Damn, but I've got to get hold of myself. Cut this shit. Need to get myself out on a court is what I need to do. Lose myself in a game. That always clears the old head. Puts things in perspective. Makes me realize I'm making mountains out of molehills. Ellen is no more a drunk than I am, and my kids are no better or worse than the next man's. Just kids growing up and finding their way is all.

'Courts six and fifteen are open,' Cindy is saying, frowning down at the sign-up sheet spread out in front of her as if it's an engineering blueprint of bewildering complexity.

She's not that bright, Cindy. That's why we gave her the job. Put someone that's bright and beautiful in there and you've got problems. I know. I already tried. I had bruised male egos calling me at the office and jealous wives calling Ellen at home. Ellen came down and took one look and that was the end of brains and beauty at the club.

I start to say give us fifteen; it's an end court and that means less people I'll have to apologize to later, explain away Jack's clothes and the way he carries on. But then I remember how I felt a moment ago with disappointment eating me alive, and how before that I'd already decided to give Jack his head, and I say, 'Put us on six,' because it's the stadium court.

'Do we get to play now?' Jack asks, coming upright from where he's been leaning, both elbows on the counter, his eyes on a level with Cindy's cleavage.

'You get to play,' I say, and laugh. I don't see the clothes he's wearing anymore, and my anger over the parking space is gone. All I see is a guy who, unless he's gone to sleep on himself, is the best player around. One who, with his wild and wonderful ways, is capable of blasting the demons out of my head, not just for a few hours but maybe for good, and I can't wait to get started.

FOUR

I'm just coming in from the Pro Court, telling Cindy which member's account to charge my lesson to, when my voice is drowned out by the bass beat of a heavy-metal rock band coming from the parking lot.

'What the . . . ?' I splutter, and stride to the Pro Shop door. I get there just in time to see a little red convertible streak into Austin's parking space and Austin himself braking hard to avoid hitting it.

'Who the hell . . . ?' I explode, thinking I'm going to have to chew out some brain-dead Junior.

'Hal . . . ' I hear Cindy yell, and I see she's holding the phone out in my direction. But I've got the door open now and am engulfed, infuriated, by the earthshaking volume of noise.

'Turn the fucking thing down, asshole,' I bellow, knowing he can't possibly hear me, yet venting anyway. But I say it a fraction of a second after the guy leaning against the car reaches in and turns the noise off, and it's my words that are left hanging in the sudden quiet.

Embarrassed, I hesitate, torn between going to tell the moron, whoever he is, to get out of Austin's space, and wanting to act as if nothing happened. I mean, screaming obscenities at the guests is hardly what's expected from the Club Pro. Especially when there's kids straggling in from all directions for their 10 a.m. clinic.

I'm spared further indecision by the sight of Austin himself sauntering towards the guy with a friendly kind of attitude, which is surprising given the circumstances, and I think, Uh-oh, time to keep my mouth shut, and beat a hasty retreat to my office just off the Pro Shop. I leave the door ajar, though, so I can see if they come in together. I mean, is this someone Austin actually knows, or is it just some passerby asking are these public courts, or looking for directions, whatever . . . ?

Must be someone Austin knows, though I'm finding that hard to believe. They've just passed my door and they're talking in a friendly kind of way, laughing . . . That's a relief. Means I won't have to be the one to tell the guy his clothes are not acceptable at this club. But hey, if he's Austin's friend, maybe his guest, that lets me off the hook.

I told him once – Austin, that is – that one of the things I don't like about my job is enforcing the rules to our older, Very Important Members. I mean, they don't take it kindly when a young guy like me tells them they can't play on the clay courts in the shoes they're wearing. Or that they have to sign in their guests *before* they go out – sneak out – to the courts.

'Austin will hear about this . . . ' They glower, making me feel like an overzealous schoolboy when I chase them down with the tab they should have signed in the Pro Shop.

'Hal,' Austin said with the patience I've come to admire, when I explained my reluctance, 'rules are important because they simplify everything. Not just here, but everywhere . . . life in general. They're there to help you, the club, the members. That's why we have so many. And that's why new members are required to sign their agreement to them before we let them in. They don't like it . . . give you a hard time . . . remind them of that.'

Yeah, right, I remember thinking. I can just see the expression on their faces when I tell them to go read the rule book.

As if reading my mind, Austin said, 'What would you do, Hal, if someone came in here insisting that three balls be used for serve instead of two?'

'OK,' I said, feeling stupid, 'I got it. I'd tell them it was against the rules.'

'Right,' he said, slapping me on the shoulder. 'And, Hal . . . I want you to know that when members call and complain to me about you . . . ' He smiled. 'Yes, they do call. I always back you up.'

I'd felt a lump forming in my throat when he said that and I swallowed hard to clear it, all the while mumbling something about appreciating his belief in me. A belief no one who knew me back when I was on the tour would have shared. A belief I didn't share myself – or lost somewhere along the way – till Austin hired me.

I remember I'd been sitting on a plane going somewhere (in my later years on the tour I hardly ever knew where I was going, just that there was a tournament down there somewhere), and I was staring vacantly ahead at nothing when I saw the curtains of the first-class cabin part and a tall, distinguished-looking guy came easing his way past the stewardess and her cart, stopped beside me, and said, 'I saw you board. Do you mind if I sit here for a while? I'd like to talk to you.'

I'd looked around thinking, Does he mean me? Must. The seats next to me are empty. I was confused. I mean, who was he? And what did he want to talk to me about?

'My name's Austin Sinclair,' he said, reaching out to shake my hand. 'We share the same hometown. Went to the same high school you did, way back when. I've been following your career.'

'You have?' I said, thinking there hadn't been a whole lot for him to follow lately. I mean, it had been a while since I made the headlines.

'How old are you now?' he asked. 'Twenty-eight? Twenty-nine?'

'Twenty-nine,' I said, carefully omitting that the big three-oh was only a week away.

'That's perfect,' he said. 'Here's what I have in mind.'

And he proceeded to tell me about a tennis club he was getting ready to open back home. Said it was going to be the best. Drew the court layout on a napkin. Described all the other facilities. And all the time I was thinking, So what? What's your club got to do with me? And I guess he saw me wondering because he capped his fountain pen and said, ' . . . and it occurs to me there'll come a day' – and he'd looked at me over the top of his glasses – 'when you're going to have enough of going up and down in airplanes. And when that time comes,' he'd gone on, 'why . . . I'd like you

45

to consider coming to work for me . . . ' And he'd beamed, adding, 'As Head Pro.'

I remember staring at him in confusion, my mind a whirl of contradictory thoughts and emotions. While part of me was flattered that a total stranger would seek me out with a job offer, another part was going, Whoa, just a minute here. What's he getting at? Is he suggesting I don't have it any-more? That it's time to pack it up? That hurt. I mean, shit, I was still winning some, just not the big ones. And if that was the case, why would he want to hire me? Besides, wouldn't Head Pro mean running the whole ball of wax? What did I know about setting up tournaments, social functions, hiring, firing, supplies, maintenance? Zip, that's what. I'm a tennis player, not a manager. I wouldn't know where to begin.

I shook my head. 'You've got the wrong man,' I said firmly, not wanting to get into it, come off sounding defen-sive. 'That's not my style at all. Sorry.'

'Your name means a lot back home,' Austin persisted. 'There's not many of us ever got our names in the national news. On television. You'd be a great asset. Bring up mem-bership. And you're picture-perfect on the court . . . '

Yeah, I thought, just not in my head, where it counts.

'Look,' I said, trying to be patient. 'I like my life the way it is, OK? It's a great life. I get to travel all over the world. Meet interesting people . . . celebrities . . . I have a lot of fun. And I don't know anything about the workings of a club.'

'You know a hell of a lot more than you think you do,' he said reassuringly. 'You and I both know tennis teaches more than just how to play a game. And with all those years on the court . . . in and out of every conceivable kind of club . . . Don't underestimate yourself.' He stood up. 'I think you're a natural. We'd start you out on a six-month trial period. If you don't like it, you leave. If we don't like you, we'll ask you to leave. And I'll be there every step of the way till you get your momentum going. Give it some thought, OK?' And handing me his card, he disappeared back into first class.

Not in this lifetime, I thought, watching the curtain swing shut behind him. Go find some other sucker. It'll be a cold day in hell before I'll open up a can of worms like that. Too much responsibility for me. And punching a pillow against the headrest, I'd gone to sleep.

But over the next few weeks, his offer kept coming back, seducing me with the promise of some stability in my life, of belonging somewhere, and I began to think, no more hauling around an ambition I can't live up to anymore. No more sweating the draws. No more hanging around airports. No more shit food and cheap hotels. No more suitcases full of stinking, dirty clothes. And no more tormented indecision: Should I quit now or play just a couple more to see if I can't find, regain, what I started with? And always opting for a couple more because . . . well, shit, it was just easier.

Things moved fast when I did make the call, and next thing I know I'm teaching housewives and little kids how to hold a racquet and liking it! I found that taking charge and running things suits me just fine. And I like the admiration and respect I get from the members when they see my trophies and awards, the photos, the news clippings all hanging in my office. It brings home to me that none of those years on the road were wasted as I'd begun to fear.

47

Like Austin said, I learned a lot more than I thought I had, and what I know I pass on to others. And it blows my mind to this day how a stranger could come along, point me in a whole new direction, and have the fit be so perfect, I swear you could hear the click.

And I discovered, once I got over the feeling of coming home with my tail between my legs, that this town I'd been so fired up to put behind me is one hell of a nice place to live. I've got the best wife in the world. A second son on the way. A nice house. And I hope I never see the inside of a plane again as long as I live. Just like seeing them, little noiseless specks of silver, high in the sky over the Pro Court.

I look at my watch, scramble to my feet. Five to ten. Time for my clinic. 'Who was the guy with Austin?' I ask Cindy, passing her desk.

'His last name's Winston,' she says, looking at the sign-up sheet. 'Jack, I think Austin called him. He's cute!'

'If you say so,' I say, while my mind's turning over the guy's name. Jack Winston . . . ? Rings a bell . . . And then I remember. 'He went to high school with Austin,' I say. 'I remember seeing his name on some of the plaques hanging in the gym. Must be a hell of a player. Has to be. He beat Austin as often as Austin beat him. Well, that explains a lot. All that noise out there. The outfit. He's putting Austin on. Doing a "Class Reunion" kind of thing.'

'He sure had Austin acting strange,' Cindy says.

'Strange? How, strange?'

She shrugs. 'I don't know. Austin looked kind of like he was in a daze. He even started talking to himself.'

'You're nuts, Cindy,' I say, picking up a basket of balls and my racquet and heading for the door.

I make it a point never to discuss Austin, the members, or anyone who works here. I found out early on that idle remarks quickly turn to gossip, and gossip turns vicious with innuendo. The sentence left hanging. The lift of an eyebrow. But she's made me curious with that last remark. Austin looked dazed? Was talking to himself? Probably means nothing. Just an airhead's brand of chitchat. Doubtless Austin was preoccupied like he always is. I just hope he didn't spot something out of line that falls under my authority.

'Hal,' Cindy calls.

I turn.

'You're cute, too,' she smirks, fluttering her eyelashes.

'I know it,' I say. 'Too bad I'm married, huh?' And feeling like a Cub Scout leader, I hustle my little band of chattering kids out to the Pro Court.

FIVE

Following behind Austin out to the courts is making me feel like I just landed in some Twilight Zone time warp where the years I just joked about haven't happened. How could they when Austin, from the rear in tennis shorts, is still the same long-legged, tight-assed, slender kid I followed onto so many courts way back long ago?

Sure, the clothes are different. Nowadays Austin wears the best money can buy. Stuff that has other people's names and weird-looking symbols – symbols that equal price tags – sewn all over the outside so you won't make a mistake and take them for any old piece of shit or the wearer for less than cool.

Austin's always been like that when it comes to style. A follower, not a leader. If the right people start wearing something, he'll figure it's safe for him to do the same and then do it like he hopes nobody notices. He'll take a long time doing it, though. Make sure it's what his crowd is doing and not just some cheap fad that blew in from Hollywood. Took him four years, till he was a senior, to let his buzz cut grow out.

There wasn't any such thing as designer labels back in the

days he and his crowd took off for college. They didn't call a certain look 'preppy' either – or if they did, I never got the word. But I noticed the guys – and the girls too – that went away, came back with a different look about them. As though there was only one store in town up there and all it sold was khaki chinos, pale pink shirts, and white buckskins.

It took me a while – I don't know why, I guess I'd already lost touch with kid things – to see it was an affectation. But when I did I understood the clothes were a kind of prestigious uniform. A uniform that stamped the wearer 'College Kid.'

A lot of that crowd dress the same way now. This town is full of barrel-shaped, gray-haired men and women still dressing like campus kids. As though the clothes are all that's left to remind them of their glory days. Of a time when they felt themselves the chosen ones, members of an elite corps who believed a college degree was the only tool necessary to live the good life.

As soon as I realized what it all stood for, I went out of my way to dress different. Reverse snobbism, I guess you'd call it. But hell, I made it further without college than all of them put together – except Austin, of course – and I don't need to parade around in a damn uniform to remind myself of my glory days. I'm still living mine.

Same way I made the point of not dressing like Austin and his crowd, I stayed away from this swank club they put together on a vacant piece of land Austin foreclosed on at the 'right' end of town.

Of course, they bugged the hell out of me to join. They

51

bombarded me with offers of a charter membership at half price and free locker space and I don't know what all. But I stayed loyal to the old club in what's now the 'wrong' end of town. It's worn and it's shabby, but down there we aren't hung up on what we wear and who we're seen playing with. We go to play tennis, not name-drop. And anyway, I don't need a college degree to know that even though I might join their club, I'd never belong. I don't talk mergers and acquisitions and alumni. I talk boats and women and tennis. Pretty much in that order.

Still . . . 'I'm impressed,' I say to Austin's back. 'This is quite a place you've got here.' And I'm not bullshitting him. It is.

Has to be a good twenty courts from what I can see, and maybe there's more I can't. There are shaded walks between the courts, with groupings of tables and chairs under striped awnings. There are smooth lawns and expensive shrubs and man-made lakes and swimming pools. And towering over everything, looking strangely like Austin's own home, the clubhouse. A monolith in redwood and glass.

'Glad you like it,' he says over his shoulder, and I can see I've made him smile. 'There were times there,' he goes on, 'I thought we'd never get it off the ground.'

'I could've told you otherwise,' I say. 'There's nothing old Austin decides on doing that doesn't get done, if I remember right.'

'Yes . . . well . . . you start something, you see it through, right?'

'I guess,' I say, thinking how he started at the bottom of

the pile in that bank of his, remembering how he had but the one job at the gas station and kept it all through high school versus all the ones I had and quit.

We used to laugh back then, the rest of us, leaving him behind working while we headed for the beach, our old cars piled high with girls and more girls and beer.

'So long, Austin! Have fun, Austin!' we'd yell, peeling out from the gas pumps where he'd filled our tanks and washed down our windshields. And if we felt like shits leaving him there in the grease-monkey uniform his mother starched and pressed as though he was wearing it to the Senior Prom, we didn't let on. We laughed harder. Hey, it was his choice, wasn't it? There wasn't one of us who had more money than him, but that didn't mean we couldn't let up once in a while and have some fun, did it?

'What's this court then?' I ask, coming out from the shaded tunnel we've been walking through and seeing a sturdily built, miniature grandstand where the other courts have tables and chairs.

'This is our stadium court,' he says, his voice and eyebrows going up on the last two words as though it's something he's got to defend, something he expects me to laugh at. 'Can't call it a club if you don't have a stadium court, can you?' he goes on in the same indignant manner. 'We play our club finals here. Adults and Juniors. And we put on exhibitions . . . '

'Yeah?' I say, keeping my face bland. 'And is that what we're going to be doing? Putting on an exhibition?'

He laughs and dumps his gear on the first row of seats. 'Why not?' he says. 'We're still the best around, aren't we?'

53

And the way he's looking at me I can see he's wondering just what kind of game I'm going to give him.

I don't say anything. Just smile. Pretty soon he'll see there are some things Jack Winston can stick with and tennis is one of them.

In the silence he turns away and starts tinkering with his racquets, and again, seeing the absorbed expression on his face, the tilt of his head, I'm back in the time warp. Only it wasn't racquets he messed with then but an old lawn mower. He'd fool with that piece of shit for so long, sharpening the blades, dripping on oil, wiping this, adjusting the other – all of it done with special tools he kept in a special oil-soaked rag – he'd have us holding our breath when the time came for him to actually roll the thing out onto the grass and damn near cheering when he got it to start.

He's got three. Racquets, I mean. All of them Princes. And one at a time he's picking them up, thumping the strings against the heel of his palm, then listening, face rapt, to the sound of their tension. And watching him I'm thinking, Sweet Jesus! What can it be like to be Austin Sinclair with nothing more on your mind than the tension in your goddam racquets?

Pretty damn nice, I answer myself. Pret-ty damn nice. And even while that's going through my mind, I'm shaking my head thinking, Shit . . . is this what debt's brought you to? That you'd stand around envying the life of an old fart like Austin Sinclair. That's the kind of life you've always sneered at. The kind where one day runs into the next like an endless string of identical beads, each one with the same routine, the same office, the same house, the same faces

54

around you day after day, year after year. Come on, man, where's the challenge? The excitement?

Screw challenge, I answer myself again. And fuck excitement. Lord knows I've pursued both enough to last ten lifetimes, and look where they got me. In the red up to my ass. And at a time in my life when I thought I'd be rolling in it. Feeding it to the pigeons. And God, but I've had enough of it! I'm sick dodging people I owe. Chasing after others I think might buy. I want some peace, for Christ's sake. Want to go home nights and leave the phone on the hook.

And I'm sick to death telling lies about why I don't belong to this frigging club and why I dropped out of so many others. The truth is I'm not a member here because I can't come up with the bucks. And if you don't think that's a hard thing to admit, then how come I just stumbled when there's nothing within a hundred yards to trip over?

And still that's not the whole of it. What gets me the worst, eats me alive, is how I let what I had slip away. Let myself get into this mess when all I ever wanted was to go on living the way I brought myself up to live. The way Austin lives . . .

'Christ, Austin!' I say, saying something, anything, for the sake of saying it. Talking to stop the frenzy going on in my head.

He stops messing with his racquets and looks up sharp, startled by the exasperation in my voice, and without meaning to, I'm moving sideways. Austin has pale eyes and pale sandy lashes, and sometimes, depending on the light, he can look at you like you're something he doesn't see.

'Christ, Austin,' I say again, in front of him this time and.

with a smile behind my words. 'Times sure change, don't they? Three racquets! Do you remember the time you traded your sister's roller skates for one?'

He sighs. Looks off to the distance. 'I remember,' he says, and I can tell from the way he says it, mournfully, like I've reminded him of his mother's funeral, that walks down memory lane aren't the way to hack it with him today. He's no more going to laugh over the past than he did when it was the present. And suddenly, now he's standing here in front of me, I'm seeing him for what he is. Not the mythical PROMINENT BANKING AUTHORITY I'm always reading about, but as the aggravating son of a bitch he really is. What's surprising is that one or the other of us hasn't mellowed enough to make being around him any easier. Even more surprising is that I'd forgotten this side of him. Or that, in the remembering, I turned his irritating traits into endearing qualities, things to laugh about. Does memory play tricks, or is it me, getting old?

Now it's too late, I wish I hadn't come. Wish there'd been some other place left to go do my borrowing.

'You about ready?' he asks. He's set two of his racquets aside and he's making practice swings, going through imaginary serves, with the third.

I have to bite my tongue not to ask what in hell he thinks I'm standing here for, racquet in hand. 'I'm ready,' I say, telling myself to sit on it, reminding myself I'm fresh out of places to go borrowing, that this is the end of the line.

The Har-Tru is thick at the outer edges of the court where the sweepers, making their turns, have left it in drifts, and I like the shush of it underfoot. I've grown blasé about a lot of things in my life, too damned preoccupied to notice others, but walking out onto a freshly rolled clay court, its lines swept clean and white, still turns me on.

In a while, every footprint, every bounce of the ball, every skid, every turn, will record itself out here as the games unfold. But right now it's blank, unmarred, a place where I can live a whole mini life, birth to death, without having to wait around a hundred years to see how I make out. I guess that's the fascination, the mystery, of sports. Doesn't matter how long you've played, how good you are, how confident. What you don't know, not till the last point's been played, is who is walking away a winner. And that's a good way to remind yourself not to make assumptions.

What I do know, good and well, is I can lose myself out there. Forget everything but the flight of the ball and what I'm going to do with it next. And when that happens things have a way of falling back into perspective. If Austin plays the way I expect him to play, I'll soon have these goddam debts, these problems, out at arm's length where I can laugh at them again instead of clogging my nights and my days like a seething swarm of maggots.

Feeling better at the thought, feeling elation and anticipation flooding me, I let out a whoop that turns old Austin's face the color of his stupid-looking hat and take off for the backcourt.

SIX

'Hey! Get back here,' I call after Jack, seeing him go whooping off to the baseline like a penned-up horse just let out to pasture. 'We haven't spun for serve yet.'

He puts himself in reverse, chugs backwards, and without touching the net, vaults to my side.

'Christ,' I splutter, stumbling to get out of his way, 'don't you ever plan on growing up?'

His eyebrows disappear into the grungy-looking sweatband he's pulled down on his forehead. 'You're grown-up enough for both of us,' he says. And while I'm wondering what that's supposed to mean, he says, 'Your racquet's prettier than mine, you spin.'

'What do you want?' I ask. 'Rough or smooth?' And I know exactly how he's going to answer.

'Smooth.' He leers. 'Same way I like my women.' Just like I knew he would.

I spin the racquet in the palm of my hand and hold it out for him to read, and while he does, tilting it this way and that, making it obvious he needs glasses, I wonder how he is with his women. Probably screws them the same way he does everything else, I decide. With a lot of noise. A lot of gusto. A lot of laughter. Probably does it with mirrors and Polaroid cameras and has them doing things to him I've only read about. Things, from the very first, Ellen thought animal-like and disgusting and refused to consider.

'I got it,' Jack says, bringing me out of his bedroom. 'It's smooth.' And he's back on his side of the net.

'I'll give you a break,' he calls over his shoulder. 'I'll let you serve.'

I hide a smile. He doesn't fool me for a minute. He wants time to loosen up and study my game. He wants to see if I'm as good as I used to be, and boy, is he in for a surprise. I'm not nearly as good as I used to be. I'm a whole lot better.

Feeling expansive, in control, I send the first ball skimming across the net and settle down to enjoy the warm-up.

I feel a smile working its way up my face, the knot in my stomach loosening, fading away, and excitement rushing in to take its place.

A lot of things have disappointed me over the years, left me jaded, but never tennis. All I have to do is walk onto a court with a good racquet in my hand, a good opponent across the net, and I feel like I'm coming home. I forget I'm Austin Sinclair. Old Austin, as I know I'm called, President and CEO. Member of this and founder of the other. Husband. Father. And all the other layers I've piled on myself to become what I am. On a court, I'm stripped down to the basics. I just am. Period.

And when the game is over, if the play has been good enough, demanding enough, I'll carry that feeling of directness with me for a while, take it into other areas of my life, and things will seem easier, simpler, while it lasts.

Tennis is the one thing, the only thing, I refused to give up for Ellen, though God knows I had to fight for it. Had to again this morning. She . . . But no. I'm not getting into it. Ellen is one of the things I refuse to bring with me to the courts.

Doesn't look to me like Jack's changed too much tennis-wise. Not from the way he's gliding around down his end, he hasn't. He looks like he always did, like a big graceful cat. A cat that knows it's got style. That roars its displeasure over weak shots. Preens and struts on good ones.

Nothing has ever come easy to me. Maybe I've got that backwards. Maybe it's seeing Jack again reminds me how everything came so easy to him. The tennis. The women. The success . . .

Two guys came to our neighborhood one time to play a match. Don't ask me why, they weren't the kind that belonged in our end of town and I don't expect they even saw us, a grimy bunch of kids hanging around the sidelines. But unintentionally they taught us how this game is supposed to be played. When they finished, one of them gave Jack his racquet. Just like that, tossed it to him as he came off the court. And Jack took a couple of practice swings and boom! The talent was there, all ready and waiting to come out.

It was different with me. In the first place, nobody gave me a racquet and it was weeks before I got my hands on one with enough string in it to hit a ball. And in the second, it took me hundreds – make that thousands – of hours on a backboard for the strokes to come out of me in painful, elusive inches.

'You ready?' Jack calls, and I put a ball in the net, wondering how I could have let my mind wander so far back in time when what I'm supposed to be doing here is concentrate!

'Just a couple more . . . ' I call.

'As many as you want, baby,' he calls back. 'As many as you want.' And the ball is flying back and forth between us again in beautiful deep, even strokes, doing our talking for us. Showing us both where our tennis has been all these years.

'Some . . . ' he'd said when I asked if he'd been playing any lately. Some? If I didn't know better, I'd swear he'd been playing around the clock, his shots are that good. That powerful. That precise.

Course, a warm-up is not a game. The world is full of people that look like goddam professionals in a warm-up. Like Wimbledon's about to see a new star, their form's so good. But start a game with them and you soon see that's all they've got. Form. Just like the affluent-looking guys, Brooks Brothers head to toe, that come surging into my office acting like they invented money, then disappoint me the minute they open their mouths. There's nothing in their heads but wishful thinking, and everything else is just show. And if you don't have it in the head, then all the form and all the clothes and all the talk in the world aren't going to make it happen, and all you'll ever be is a pretty sight to behold. Not a winner.

Jack has always had it in his head. In his belief in himself. And if he hasn't drank and screwed it all away, if that gut of his doesn't drag him down, if he doesn't decide he'd sooner put on a show, then I'm going to have the pleasure today of beating someone who could actually beat me.

I don't return the next ball. I stop it with my racquet instead and stuff it in my pocket. I look at my Rolex. Ten-thirty.

'How about it?' I call, holding up two balls, showing him I'm ready to serve.

'Sock 'em to me,' he answers, making a big show of backing up and crouching low to receive.

I bounce the ball a couple of times. 'You're sure you're up for this?' I call, wanting to put a little doubt in his mind, get him a little edgy. 'I mean, that gut of yours isn't going to drag you down, is it?'

He laughs and nods the way a person who hasn't heard what you've said does and stays the way he is, crouched low, rocking sideways, ready to go either way.

I notice he's standing wide. Too wide for the singles court, and I suspect he's been playing a lot of doubles lately, so I aim for the T of the center line and let it fly. The serve is so true I hear it nudge the tape, but I don't go in after it. It's way too early for that, especially on clay, and why wear myself out before I see how well he's going to handle himself?

I see him pivot, his right shoulder and his racquet go back, way back, then boom . . . the ball is back on my side, as nice a shot as any I've seen. I send it crosscourt to his forehand, making him change direction, and get myself back in the center, ready to go either way, fast. He scorches it down the line to my backhand so deep, I have no choice but to lob. I get good spin on it, though, and it thuds down just inside his baseline, then takes off in a bounce so high, he'd need a ladder to handle it, and the point is mine.

All my life I've worked at keeping my thoughts off my face and I do now, but it isn't easy. First points count like game points to me. Something I have to win. Something that shows the other guy who's boss. I take the next two points, one with an ace, and I'm just beginning to think it's going to be a piece of cake, a disappointment even, when he hits a crosscourt and gets into the game.

'Forty-fifteen,' I call, knowing damn well he knows the score but wanting to remind him who has the upper hand.

I should've kept my mouth shut. I fault the first ball of my next serve and bite my tongue not to curse out loud. I see him creeping in, expecting less power on the second, so I fling it up, then let it bounce. The toss was fine, but why not befuddle him a little? Make him wait. Get him tense.

In earlier days I might have treated the second serve like a first. Given it all I had. But I've played too long now to take a chance and I've learned to conserve myself. Forty-eight is no age to throw away points, especially in this kind of heat, so I toss it again and slice the ball and it flies off my racquet like a saucer and bounces like one too. And then I'm staring, slack-jawed, at Jack diving in, skidding down on one knee and taking the ball at the top of its bounce in an overhead so lethal and unexpected, I can't believe what I'm seeing. The ball skids off the baseline at my feet and wedges itself into the fence behind me where I'd like to fling my racquet, I'm that disconcerted. Instead, acting like it's the kind of play I look at every day, I march to the fence and dislodge the ball, his shout of triumph loud in my ears.

Goddammit, but that's unnerving, that kind of play. What does he think this is, a circus? But he's shown me something there. Shown me he's still a high-risk player and an exhibitionist just like he always was, counting on luck. And everybody knows, or should by the time they reach his age, you can only count on luck so many times. So . . . that gives me my game plan. I'm going to be able to outsteady him as I always did.

I keep him waiting, bouncing the ball, while I decide how I want to play it. I think I'll go for an ace. Then think, Play it safe. Then, Shit! Go for it! It's early days yet and you're not that old, for chrissakes . . .

I take the point and the game and, not wanting his trivial chatter to disarm me, take away from my concentration, I stall to see which side of the court he's going to use for the changeover, then take the opposite, keeping my face impassive all the way.

SEVEN

The flavor of the day alters, shifts, when I see Austin holding up two balls, signaling he's ready to begin. I feel myself tighten. Am surprised at a sudden rush of adrenaline through my heart, my knees. Playtime is over.

Hey! I get stern with myself. Quit that! This is no championship and that guy down there is no Becker. That's old Austin, remember?

Maybe so, but this is one match I've got to win. Want to get myself as high in Austin's esteem as I can get before I hit him up for a loan, and he's no more the lanky kid I used to be able to intimidate than I'm the Pope. He's a grown man now. A guy who's manhandled everything he's touched, and don't tell me that's not going to show up in his game.

I watch him wind up for that studied serve of his, a serve that looks like he's practiced it hundreds of times in front of a mirror, and I'm not fooled. Austin's a powerful man. He knows how to put his weight behind his shots and he knows how to use his wrist and he knows, better than anyone I ever played, how to disguise where he's going to put the ball.

Watching him, you'll read a backhand and turn for it, only to see the ball bounce to your forehand and go flipping off over the doubles line. So what you do is, you shuffle around during his toss, let him think you've outguessed him and know exactly which way he's going. You try to make him change his mind. Lose some concentration. Take away some of his power. Force a fault or at least a tentative shot. And mostly none of it works.

Austin doesn't scare easily. He knows where he's going, and the Radio City Rockettes, high-stepping it naked, won't budge him an inch. Still . . . he never got many past me before and he doesn't now.

That first return eases the tension out of me and I settle down to enjoy myself. Austin might be good, might have a few tricks up his sleeve I don't know about yet, but I haven't exactly been sitting around whistling Dixie these past thirty years, and we'll see. We'll just see . . .

I break a sweat and feel my body cooling, my muscles loosening. Feel myself growing lighter on my feet and I'm thinking, Man, but this is the life, isn't it? What else matters? Nothing. Only now. This minute. That ball coming at me. My body doing exactly what I expect it to do. My head free and clear of everything but the point I'm playing.

And how about old Austin down there! Not your hotshot Bank President now, is he? Not a turtle hiding inside its shell either. Or a pain in the ass. Now he's just a guy like me, lost in what he's doing. Smiling. Happy. Both of us taking pleasure in the other's ability to give as good as he gets. Both making the other think, sweat, work. Just like the good old days.

The essence of those days is here now so strong I can taste it. So strong I'm constantly surprised at the clay under my

66

feet, the slower bounce of the ball, when what I'm remembering is cement. I felt it in the warm-up first when the sound of the ball flying back and forth between us was as precise and steady as a metronome ticking. As familiar as yesterday. I guess it's something we brought with us.

'Remember how we used to go for a hundred strokes apiece without stopping?' I'd called out to him.

'I remember,' he'd said, his eyes never leaving the ball. 'Did we ever make it?'

'Don't know. You couldn't count that high.'

He'd laughed and I'd felt like I'd given us both a present. Austin doesn't laugh easily.

Too bad we let so many years go by. What a waste of good tennis. I mean, shit, it's not like either one of us went away somewhere. We've both been right here all the time.

Did I say old Austin can mix up his shots? Disguise them? Well, let me tell you, I can too. Look at what I've got coming at me here. A sliced second serve, angled to spin high out over the sidelines, only I'm not going to let it. I'm going in on it, and even though that's going to leave a whole lot of court wide open, it isn't going to matter. Austin's way down there back of his baseline waiting to see which way I'm going to go, down the line or crosscourt. I'd give a lot to look at his face when he sees what I'm about to do, but it's going to take every bit of concentration I've got as well as split-second timing, so I'll have to pass on Austin's face.

Often when I'm playing someone as good as Austin and I'm pulling some of my choicer numbers out of the bag, I'm reminded of those guys who came to our court that time. I wish there was a crowd of youngsters standing around here now, watching us the way we watched them. In my mind they're here, those kids, only I don't ignore them. I talk to them. Teach them what I know.

'Watch close,' I'm telling them now. 'This isn't something you're likely to see twice in a lifetime, and the doing's going to be faster than the telling, so don't go blinking your eyes. Now, see how the spin on that serve is bouncing the ball high. And see how, instead of staying back, letting it drop, I've skidded my way in under it while it's still on its way up? Now, if I was a mite smaller – say, the height I'd be down on one knee, like so – I could treat that sucker like an overhead and slam it away, right? OK then. Let's do it and see what old Uncle Austin down there can do about it!'

The old uncle watches the ball kick up the dust at his feet, his racquet a useless weapon in his hand, and I'm whooping it up with the kids, wishing they weren't imaginary kids but real ones. And more than that, that they were my sons, the two that got into tennis before their mother moved with them out of state. And while I'm doing all that wishing, Austin gets on with the next point and takes it.

'Game,' he calls, trying not to look too pleased with himself, and I'm glad because when I get to thinking about my kids, I know it's time to stop thinking altogether. Nothing in this world'll tear me apart, make me lose my concentration faster, than letting them into my mind where, superimposed over all the good times, are the looks of betrayal and confusion I saw in their eyes when, one at a time, I had to let them go to places they didn't want to go . . . to stepfathers they didn't want to know. Jesus! Makes me feel like a monster. A traitor. Makes me think that being

68

one of my kids, being loved by me, is a one-way ticket to hell.

I head in for my towel hanging on the end of the net and a swallow of water and out the corner of my eye I see Austin, all business, stalking down the opposite side of the court, passing up both. Austin's back in his shell and he's not about to let up on himself and have a little fun. Austin's out to play a professional game of tennis and he's not going to chat around with me on the changeovers. Might take away from his concentration, right? Might make him appear human and normal like the rest of us, right again? Right.

Have it your way, baby, I think. Stand around out there in the sun and fry. Me, I'm coming in for shade and water and a towel every chance I get. Going to put back in what I'm sweating out, and that's not gamesmanship either. Not like your cheap shot earlier about my weight. Save that shit for your regulars. You ought to have remembered I'm immune to psyche-outs. Know that nothing and nobody gets into my head without my express say-so.

At the same time I'm mentally lecturing Austin, I'm keeping my eye on the mixed doubles on the next court. I know, remember, one of the couples and I'm wondering if they aren't about ready for a new boat. I'm also wondering why otherwise normal, sane-looking men and women would put themselves through the grief of playing with each other.

I did that once. Played with my wife, I mean. One time I did. And then never again.

The way I see it, mixed doubles, at the club level anyway, is either two guys, dead serious, out to win, and two women thinking they're out for a social event, swapping recipes and hairdressers across the net. Or else you've got the reverse, two outstanding women players – the kind that can take games off me – caught in the age-old conflict of wanting to win and not making their slow-moving, bookish husbands look bad while they're doing it. And what can that add up to but four very angry people going home to make big, big trouble for one another?

In this case, 'Yours . . . !' squeals the little wife, cellulite aquiver, after she's scampered in front of her husband to poach a shot that's clearly his – a net shot at that – then chickened out.

Caught off guard, the poor bastard tries running backwards, wrenches himself around to go forward, howls in pain as he dislocates a part of himself, keeps on running anyway – doing his best – only to run smack into the wife who's decided to go for it after all.

'Jesus Christ!' he howls, and his racquet follows after the ball.

The little wife, cheeks pink with indignation, eyes aglitter, very purposefully leans her racquet against the net, glares at it – daring it to fall over – then, plump hands on plump hips, advances on her husband.

'You ought to be ashamed of yourself, Rick,' she hisses, like he's two years old. 'Behaving like that in front of Claire and Steve . . . humiliating me . . . Don't you know this is a GAME?'

Thinking, Spare me, God, I pick up my racquet and mince out on the court in a fair imitation of the indignant lady.

It's lost on Austin. Down his end he's making a show of nonchalance, idly pacing the court, keeping himself psyched, stopping every now and then to gaze thoughtfully off to the distance, telling himself he's got a game, got the lead . . . and games turn into sets . . .

Don't count on it kid, I'm thinking, picking up balls to stuff in my pockets, then finding out too late I don't have pockets. Jesus Christ, why don't running shorts have pockets? And why didn't I think of that when I was putting them on? Because I was too busy thinking how they'd freak Austin, that's why.

'You want to take a couple?' he calls, magnanimity itself.

'Hell, no,' I say, and rip off an ace.

Urgent with delight, I wheel sideways into the left court and whack in another!

'Son of a bitch,' I holler, 'but I'm cooking today!'

And damn me if I don't knock out another. Ace, I mean. And there's old Austin tromping back and forth along his baseline acting cool, applauding my serves by thumping a hand against his racquet each time one of them whips up the dust in his service square. And I know what he's thinking.

He's thinking, That's Jack for you. Showing off as usual. Going for broke. Playing the exact same way he did when he was a kid. And he's telling himself, Don't sweat it! Let him think he's eighteen again. Let him waste himself early. Applaud him! Encourage him. He can't keep it up. Sooner or later he'll get too cocky . . . try for too much . . . just like he always did . . . And when he does I'll be there, strong and ready to outsteady him just like I always did.

And, 'I've got news for you, Austin,' I'm singsonging back under my breath while I'm taking my time on my next serve, bouncing the ball like I'm thinking up some wickedly

71

cunning strategy. 'I can, too, keep it up. Oh, yes indeed I can. A lot of things happen to a man in thirty years, and unless he's stupid, he learns from them. And, Austin, I'm not stupid. I just act that way. One of the things I've learned is patience. Do you believe that? Old Jack learning patience! I have, though. Had to. Couldn't make the kind of money I've made – or the women – if I was in a hurry – now, could I? Fact is, I learned to take my time a long time ago. Learned to keep them at a distance. What I do is, I torment. Imply that what I've got may be more than what they're used to. More than they can handle. I tell them to go away and think it over. I hold off my close till they're closing for me, yanking out their checkbooks, ripping off their clothes, whichever . . . And what I've learned in life, I bring to the court, so watch it, Austin! You may see me stomping around down here like Big Chief Running Mouth, but don't assume I'm still the kid I used to be, rushing in for the kill without first setting a trap, though I'll go out of my way to let you think I am. Does this fourth ace tell you anything?'

'Great serves,' he calls, gathering up the balls I've sent down his end and faking a smile. 'You're playing like . . . like Agassi!'

I hang my head, shuffle my feet. 'Shucks,' I say, 'warn't nothing. Soon's I get warmed up some, I'll do a mite better . . . '

EIGHT

'One-three,' I say, showing Jack and the idiots on the next court – people I thought intelligent until I saw them give up on their own game in favor of watching ours – that being down two games is not the least bit threatening to me.

It isn't. I'll catch up. I'm up for serve now and I'll hang on to it, break his the next to make us even, then start building my own lead. No way in hell am I going three sets today. Not this time of year in this kind of heat. Don't even know if I have the stamina for it anymore, it's been so long since anyone's taken me that far. I won't let them. I've been around the game too long for that kind of nonsense.

The fact is, I've learned to play tennis the way I deal in business. Maybe I've got that backwards. Maybe what actually happened is that I learned to do business the way I play tennis. Either way, the strategy is the same: I do my homework! Study every facet of who and what I'm dealing with and then I settle back and keep them playing and/or talking long enough for their weaknesses to surface. When they do, and they always do, I'm there with skills I've honed to perfection and I begin to apply the pressure. Gently at first, so they don't know I've caught on, then with growing insistence, I probe at one soft spot, pick at it until it's laid bare, then move on to the next. Doesn't take long for their confidence to falter and doubt to set in. Keep at it a little longer, toy with them, and I can sit back and watch them fall apart all by themselves. On the court I see a string of unforced errors. In the office I hear a stream of useless, mumbled words.

So, no thank you kindly. No three sets for me today. In another hour or so when the sun is like a blowtorch in the heavens and the humidity thick and heavy as lamb's wool, I plan on being in the club lounge on possibly my second very cold beer.

But Jesus, he's getting on my nerves with all his rambling chitchat and dawdling between games. Damn well he knows he's not supposed to be going in to towel off every time the mood takes him. If he wasn't ahead, I'd swear he was pulling some cheap-shit gamesmanship on me like those assholes that kneel to retie a shoelace or go hysterical arguing line calls every time they fall behind.

I'm tempted to tell him to move his ass, only I know better. Tell him that and he'll use my impatience against me, slow himself down even more . . . Instead I wander off to the backcourt, bouncing a ball in front of me as I go. No sense looking like 'Anxious Austin' poised to serve into a vacant court. Only makes him look the more laid-back by comparison, and I hate setting myself up for comparisons.

I examine the shrubs back there behind the fence and make mental notes to tell Hal that Grounds Maintenance needs to mulch again. And while they're there, to get rid of that moldering Coke cup and the other crap our prestigious

74

members feel free to sling around all over the grounds, as though their dues include 'trashing' privileges.

Anyway, I keep my back turned on Jack another good minute, wanting to keep him waiting, give him a taste of his own medicine, then turn to face the courts, and he's only just taking off for his baseline, sauntering there with that rolling, fat-calved walk of his. And moving so slow, you'd think he was the fade-out of a movie and any minute the words THE END are going to write themselves across his backside – a place I'd like to slam my racquet.

Thank God for my serve. True, it may not look as spectacular as his. Nobody's does. But the years I spent perfecting it paid off and now it's my most trusted weapon, there when I need it for as long as I need it. It won't fade on me as his soon will, and I can force a lot of weak returns off it while I wait for him to come down off that cloud he's playing on and that smug grin to come off his face.

Like that one right there! Wide to his forehand. Might as well have been an ace for all the play he got off it – a return so weak, he's lucky it made it over the net – so feeble, he set me up for a put-away.

And now I've got him scrambling around trying to figure which way I'm going with this next one. Fact is, I'm not going any which way with it. I'm going right at him. Going for his crotch and let's see him try and run around that.

Well . . . you do what you can. He's contorted himself around it and it's coming back, a short-angled shot that's got me scrambling, but one I can handle and at least now I'm making him work. I'm not standing around like some feebleminded beginner watching the ball dig holes in the court around me like I did when he first came up for serve. The problem then was I'd forgotten that serve of his. The speed of it. The accuracy. The way he looks executing it. I tell you, serving, Jack is a sight to behold, like those slow-motion frames they use to illustrate how-to tennis books. Flawless! And like a fool I'd stood there choked with envy as though I was a ten-year-old kid again and not a guy who outranked him many times.

But for now I need to forget Jack and his almighty serve and everything else about his game and bear down on him. I need to hang tough and run him and his fat and his forty-eight years until he's begging for mercy.

He will. He has to. The player hasn't been born that can keep up the kind of play he's showing me now. Not from this early on in the match, he can't. He's peaked too early is what he's done. Way too early. There's still too much tennis ahead of him to hang on to it. Too much time for his head to fill up with other things.

I know. I've been there. I've done it myself and seen it happen a thousand times to others, from beginners right through the pros. You start out and it's like everything you ever learned suddenly falls into place. You can almost hear the click. And you're thinking, Will you look at me! Did you ever see anything so easy? So effortless? Man, I'm a smoking terror! Doesn't matter where he puts the ball, how hard he hits it, I'm there ahead of him, playing like I always knew I could. And will you look at what I'm sending back! Stuff he can't get close to. This is how I've always known I could play and now it's happening point after point, game after game. Pretty soon I'll have myself a set . . . then another . . . If he doesn't wake up and figure out some way to play me, I will. If he doesn't get a rhythm of his own going, I will. If I can keep this up myself, I will. Course I can keep it up! What's to stop me? All I have to do is keep on doing what I'm doing and that's . . . Well, let's see here, just what is it I'm doing today that's so special? So different?

You're asking for trouble wondering how. You start asking questions, looking for answers, start trying to do what's already coming naturally, and you're going to get in your own way. Get tentative. And that's when the shit starts hitting the fan.

But I learned a long time ago not to let that happen. First off, I won't let myself think, ask questions. And second, I've learned to groove myself, to build, so I peak when I want to, at a place where I know I can hold on to it and carry it through to the end.

Haven't I said the whole damn game's in the head? And doesn't a man play a sport the way he lives his life? Sure he does. You can't live a lie on a tennis court. Not for long anyway. There, sooner or later, the truth surfaces.

'Live for the moment!' has been Jack's modus operandi as far as I can tell. And where has it gotten him? Has he ever built anything lasting? Not him. In and out of all those marriages. In and out of the same amount of boatyards. Kids scattered all over the state and to hell and gone. Where's the strength? The roots? The staying power? You tell me . . .

'Go for the long haul' has been my motto. Along those lines anyway. Something to do with tenacity and stability and never giving up. Not ever. All qualities Jack has failed to master. So let him have his moment because that's all it'll ever be – a moment. And let him strut and crow and draw a crowd. I can bide my time, wait him out, build my strengths. And at the end of the day it'll be me showing him and the clowns on the next court and the ones drifting by and staying to watch what it takes to win a match and build a valid life.

So I tell myself until he scrambles to catch me and brings the score to deuce. So I continue to tell myself when he does it again, then takes two consecutive points for the game. And now I'm thoroughly pissed . . .

NINE

The mixed doubles, their game finished, have drifted over in a tentative kind of way, ready to back off quick if Austin shows any sign of annoyance at their presence, but he doesn't and that surprises me.

Austin plays OK in front of a crowd; his Junior wins, his rankings, tell you that. But he was always happier, played better, when no one was around to watch, not even his family. Not that they came out often and never together. How could they? Somebody had to stay home to mind the house and CLEAN, didn't they? But even one parent, not making a sound, only their eyes following the play like they were reading a newspaper, was more than Austin could handle, and after a while he had them stop coming altogether.

Anyway, either he hasn't noticed we've got company or he doesn't care anymore, and pretty soon one of the guys, tired of standing – maybe not ready yet to go home where he'll play the real match – grunts himself down in the bleachers. The others, seeing he hasn't been struck dead for his boldness, trickle in and join him, the men sprawled loose on one bench, the women, three tiers away, huddled together in hissing indignation over the way their men behaved on the court.

'Love-fifteen,' Austin drones, using his racquet to scoop up the ball he's just whacked into the net and sending it back to me.

'One down, three to go,' I tell the first guy, the bold one, bouncing a ball on the rim of my racquet while I'm waiting for Austin to get back in place.

'Yeah?' he says, looking over at Austin with a kind of reverence, like he's Jesus Christ in tennis clothes. He smirks, settles his elbows on the bench behind him. 'Show me,' he says.

Hustling around the court like I'm on skates, I do. 'There's another one for you,' I tell him, and I hold up two fingers.

'Lucky . . . ' he says, watching me slit-eyed. 'You just got lucky.'

'Great get,' Austin calls, showing us all how sure of himself he is. How certain that a point is not a game and a game is not a set and that he has no worries – is just biding his time until I get so carried away with my Mr Personality routine, I'll screw up and let him wipe me off the court.

When's he going to wake up? Can't he see after all I'm showing him that I've learned to let my mouth run without ever letting it intrude on the part of my mind that's focused on the flow of the game to the exclusion of everything else?

Evidently he can't. Or won't. So all the time I'm picking off everything he can send me and keeping up with the remarks, I'm thinking, Come on, man! Get your shit together! I'm not that fucking stupid anymore. I'm a grown man. Treat me like one . . .

We're fighting over this point, both of us intent on keeping the other at the baseline and at the same time looking for a short ball to follow to net. Austin gets one and he's right there behind it, slamming down an overhead.

'Way to go, baby,' his buddy in the bleachers yells, coming to his feet. Only he says it too soon. The ball overshoots the baseline by a good couple of inches and I'm yelling, 'Out!'

'Bad luck, fella . . . ' the guy sighs, sinking back into his seat, pointedly ignoring the three fingers I'm waving in his direction.

'Love-forty,' Austin says, still playing the sport but eyeing the mark left by the ball from where he stands at the net. He sees it clear and round and undeniably long, circled by a ring I've drawn around it with my racquet, and he shrugs and ambles off looking unconcerned, but I know I'm rattling his chain.

If I had any doubts, he lays them to rest on the next point, overhitting the ball so bad, it doesn't touch the ground at all but slams into the fence behind me and stays there.

Of course, I go through my victory stomp, wave all four fingers at my friend in the stands, knowing I'm doing him a favor. Giving him me to be disgusted with instead of Austin, who's letting him down. But frankly, I'm pissed.

This isn't the kind of match I came here to play. I came here to earn something off someone I thought was my equal – on the courts, anyway – not to stomp all over him. If I'd known his tennis had gone off this badly, I'd have turned down his invitation, looked for some other way to approach him. I mean, how am I going to feel asking him for a loan if

I beat him so badly, neither one of us can look the other in the eye?

Lopsided matches suck. I hate 'em. They're an embarrassment to everyone. Austin's feeling like a jerk despite the show he's putting on, and no wonder, down five-one to a yahoo like me on his own turf. And these spectators are squirming, as embarrassed by their Number One Man's play as if they'd caught him with his pants down. And me? I'm the bad guy. The cad come to deflate Austin's pride. But hey! I'm not letting up on him. There's way too much time and way too much tennis to run through for me to start going soft. And if he was ahead, then I'd be behind, and whose face am I playing for anyway, his or mine? That's a good question. That's something I maybe ought to be asking myself with things turning out the way they are. Just what am I playing for today? The match or my survival? But Jesus . . . throw a match? That's something I've never done in my life. I wouldn't know how. I mean you play to win, don't you? Well . . . don't you?

'Goddammit, Austin, hit the frigging ball, will you!' I yell, taking my frustration out on him. 'Show me some tennis . . . '

Tell you one thing. If I was in his shoes right now, I'd chalk this set up. Whack in my serves any which way . . . let me put them away . . . then slam the door on it. Let it go. Regroup. Come up with a whole new strategy for the second set.

But I'm not Austin, and Austin's not going to let it go that easy. He's got his game plan and he's sticking to it. He aims to outsteady me every point of every game. He wants to run me legless. It isn't getting through to him that it's him doing the running. Jesus! How can he control that empire of his the way they say he does and be so stupid, so juvenile, so inflexible on a court?

Pretty soon we're at six-one, and 'You played a great set,' he says, coming in at the end of it for his first drink, his first rest since we started. 'I'd have known you were this tough, I might not have been so free with my invitation,' he goes on, flopping himself down in a chair and mopping his face.

'Thanks,' I say, already hardly able to look him in the face, and I take off to chat it up with the original foursome and a few others who've come by.

Old peddlers like me don't ever pass up a chance to say hello to people. Get names. We can't afford to, though it's been my experience the tennis crowd rarely goes in for boats – not expensive ones anyway – and vice versa. But I'm to the point where I'd be happy to sell a canoe and I'm out for names. Leads. Contacts.

Anyway, playing to a crowd always brings my game up and keeps it there, and the way Austin's playing, I need these people to stick around, else he'll drag me down to his level and turn this whole frigging match into a contest of good manners.

My dad knew how I was. 'The kid's playing Saturday,' he'd say into the phone, working his way down a dog-eared list of names he kept in his wallet. 'Why don't you come out? Give him some support . . . and hey, bring the missus . . . the kids . . . '

I'd hear excited squawks on the other end of the line. Laughter. Nobody ever turned my dad down. Not because I was playing but because the invitation always included supper at the house afterwards. And wine, homemade, from a keg he kept covered with an old tarp out in the garage. I never think of those days that the smell of my mother's cooking doesn't come with the memories. Damn if I'm not drooling now . . .

Anyway, when the time came for me to play, I'd walk out to more fans than some small towns have populations, all of them wild with enthusiasm over everything I hit and none of them knowing a serve from an overhead or an ad from a deuce, and not caring. They were there to keep their end of the bargain, cheer me on, and God help any official who got in their way.

'Hey! Go home, read the rule book,' they'd tell the umpire.

'Yeah. Go home. Go home or get lost, whatever turns you on.'

'Go get yourself some new glasses. That ball was good. Tell him, Jack . . . '

I played my heart out for them. I will for these people too. Most particularly I will for these people, seeing how they've made up their minds they don't like me. They don't like the way I'm dressed and they don't like the way I talk, and most of all, they don't like what I'm doing to their hero. I've brought out the old herd instinct, and they're set to rally round one of their own.

That's OK. That's good. Let 'em. Cracking them, bringing them over to my side, will have to be my challenge, seeing Austin's not coming through with one.

TEN

'There must be something going on in the stadium court,' Mark says at the end of our match, seeing players, their own games over, all making their way in the same direction. 'Let's check it out.'

'You've got a stadium court?' I say. 'I'm impressed.'

'You name it, we've got it,' he says, beaming the way you do when you've got something the other guy hasn't and surprises still up your sleeve. 'I told you you'd be blown away by this place, didn't I?'

'You did, and I am,' I say. 'Who's playing? Someone famous?'

'I doubt it,' he says. 'It would have been in the monthly newsletter, plastered all over the Pro Shop, if they were expecting a big name. Probably just some of the members, Austin maybe, in a really close match. Happens all the time on the weekends. We've got some great players here. Another reason for you to join.'

'Who's Austin?' I ask, hearing a burst of clapping.

'He's the guy that built this place. He owns it. Yep . . . that's him,' he says now we're close enough to see. 'The guy in the hat.' And he nods towards a tall guy serving in the near end of the court.

'He reminds me of Stan Smith,' I say admiringly, taking in not just his build but his style of play.

'He plays like him too. He's club champ, ' Mark says, beaming again as though he's just pulled Austin out of a hat for my benefit. 'Beats guys half his age. Look how he's got the other guy running. Oh, well . . . ' he sighs. 'That one was long.' And raising his voice, calls, 'Bad luck, Austin,' as though he's Austin's personal coach and best friend.

'Who's he playing?' I ask, craning for a better view of the far end of the court over the heads of the people crowded in front of me.

But before he can answer, the unseen opponent lets out a howl and I freeze. I recognize that voice. It's a voice I'd know anywhere. It's the voice of Jack Winston, my stepdad. Someone I've been going out of my way to avoid for a long time because I don't have the guts to look him in the eye. And he's playing here? This is the last place I'd have expected to see him knowing his dislike for all things correct and regimented.

'I don't know who he is,' Mark says. 'I've never seen him before.' And he frowns as though personally insulted that here's a name he can't drop. 'He can play, though, I'll give him that. That's two aces in a row he's got past Austin. No wonder the folks are trekking in. Come on, let's get a seat in the bleachers before they fill up.'

'I . . . I really can't stay that long,' I hedge. 'Got a lunch date. But you go ahead. I'll just watch from here for a while and then take off. But hey . . . thanks for having me over as your guest. It's been great. I really appreciate it.'

'My pleasure, Steve,' he says absentmindedly, his attention on the court. 'Let me know if you decide to join. I'll be glad to sponsor you.' And he takes off for the bleachers where I see him clamber up to the top row.

Every muscle in my body is tensed ready to get away from here and Jack's mocking gaze, but something seems to be keeping me rooted to the ground. I'm curious, I guess.

I've done such a good job avoiding him since our blowup, I haven't even seen him from a distance. Now, by keeping my head low, ducking behind these people in front of me, I can catch up with him, sort of, without him knowing I'm around.

He's added a pound or two, grown a beard. But otherwise he's the same old Jack. The guy I admire most on the planet.

I was eight years old when my mom married Jack and pretty disgusted at the whole situation. I thought things were cool the way they were and I didn't want a stepfather coming in to mess things up.

'I'm not gonna call you Dad,' I said, wanting him to know right off how things were going to be between us.

'That's cool,' he said. 'Jack'll do fine.'

'And I'm not gonna . . . ' And I tried to come up real quick with some other 'nots,' seeing I'd won the first round. 'I'm not gonna do nothing,' I said finally, thinking I might as well lay it all on the line. And then I watched him real close seeing how he'd take that.

'Nothing, huh?' he said. 'Well . . . then I guess your mom and I'll just go pick up the other kids and take the boat out for the day, seeing nothing's going to be happening around here. Anything we can get you before we take off?'

'Um . . . ' I stalled, my mind racing over what I could possibly say I wanted. I mean, nobody'd ever asked me that before. I'd never been left alone before.

'I'll just call a baby-sitter,' my mom said, reaching for the phone and starting to dial.

'Course,' Jack said, looking thoughtful, 'I guess a person can do nothing on a boat just as well as right here, huh, Stevie?'

'I guess they could,' I said quickly, seeing my way out of the trap I'd set for myself. 'A boat's a great place to do nothing.'

'Sometimes, though,' he went on, looking real worried, 'not often, mind you, but just every once in a while, I need help out there. I might need to ask you to steer, or maybe throw me a line. How's that going to work out if you're all tied up doing nothing?'

'No sweat,' I said. 'I can still do stuff like that. I'll probably be real good at it.'

Everything I know, fishing, sailing, calculus – yep, calculus – baseball, tennis, Jack taught me the way he taught me to handle that boat. Like it was me helping him out.

Five years later, when he and my mom split up, I felt like my world caved in.

'You can't do this to me,' I yelled at my mother. 'That's *my* dad you're throwing out. How'm I supposed to get along without him? Who's gonna be there for me? I'm gonna go live with him and don't try and stop me.'

Course, she did, and it took me a few years to forgive her

for that. But I spent a lot of time with Jack anyway, riding my bike over to see him whenever I could, calling him for help and advice through my high school years, the college years, my whole world revolving around his shouts of approval, his bear hugs at my achievements.

I'm watching him now hit a backhand crosscourt and I have to bite my lip not to let out a roar of approval at the perfect placement of his shot. A shot that leaves the other guy floundering, and once again I'm shaking my head, sickened, at how I could have ever been so stupid, so cocky, to betray Jack the way I did and then walk out of his life.

'I'm counting on you, Stevie,' he'd said, for about the fiftieth time, sitting in the car beside me outside the airport. 'You know I'd never leave town with a sixty-five-foot Orca sitting in the water waiting approval, but it's critical to get the other boat we sent to Miami ready and the crew up and running before the owners fly in Saturday. I said I'd do it, so I'll do it, but Jesus, why does it always work out this way? We go six months with hardly a nibble and then we've got two going at the same time. Anyway, Morrison knows I won't be here. Knows you'll be standing in for me to go over the new stuff. Just do everything exactly like I told you. Don't let him order any extras unless you get it in writing and don't let him tell you we've put in stuff he didn't order. Son of a bitch tries it every time. And don't go getting creative on me, promise him stuff we can't deliver, OK? Just schmooze with him, keep him happy till I get back Sunday.'

'Jack . . . Jack . . . ' I said. 'Cool it. You taught me, remember? I've been selling over a year now. I can handle it. I won't let you down. And, uh . . . don't you think it's time you stopped calling me Stevie? Come on. I'm twenty-three.'

'Christ,' he spluttered. 'With all I've got going on right now, you want me to worry about what I call you. OK. OK. Sorry. You're Steve from now on. Where were we? Yeah. Morrison. He's a weasel, Stevie . . . Steve. One of the worst I've ever come across. The kind of guy I wouldn't do business with if my back wasn't up against the wall. But we need these sales, Stevie . . . Steve. Gotta have 'em. We lose either one of these and we might as well hang it up and go sell popcorn.'

'No sweat,' I said, turning the key in the ignition. 'We'll do it. And hey, maybe I'll be able to unload the Prowler while you're gone. All forty-five feet of her.'

'You do that and I'll kiss your feet when I get back,' he said, slamming the car door and leaning in the window. 'You know what you've got to do now, right? You're gonna do it all just like I said. And one other thing, don't either one of you sign anything till I get back . . . '

'You're sounding like a broken record, Jack,' I said, and pulled away from the curb thinking he's not only sounding like a broken record, he's sounding old. Old and boring. And then I forgot him altogether thinking ahead to the next couple of days when, with the place to myself, I planned on making enough commissions to finally buy my own boat. Maybe even update my car . . .

'YOU DID WHAT?' Jack said two days later, in a tone of voice I'd never heard before, looking up from the paperwork I'd left on his desk, his face whiter than any face I'd ever seen.

'I sold the Prowler,' I said, the smile leaving my face and exasperation taking its place, thinking, Do I have to draw a picture? 'Just like I said I would,' I went on, and put my foot up on his desk. 'You can kiss my foot now.'

With a backhand swipe to my leg Jack knocked my foot off the desk and I went sprawling into the opposite wall where he advanced on me, the bill of sale in his hand. 'I told you not to let Morrison sign anything, didn't I?' he roared. 'And I told you not to sign anything, didn't I? I told you the guy was a weasel. Christ! You let him walk out of here, signed and sealed, with the Prowler? What about the Orca? Come on, Stevie, tell me you didn't . . . '

My silence confirmed his fear and he slammed his fist into the wall. 'You couldn't have! You're not that stupid. You knew the Orca was *his* boat. Who the hell else is going to want sixty-five feet of lime green interiors? What are we supposed to do with it now? Sell raffle tickets? Jesus! You've ruined me! That's it. And I know that swine Morrison's at the Yacht Club right now spreading the word about how he got himself the deal of the century. Why not? You made it so easy for him. All he had to do was wait till I turned my back. And I trusted you! I trained you! I believed in you . . . !'

I tried to wet my lips in preparation for my defense, but my mouth was so dry I couldn't get out a word, though my head churned with good, valid reasons why I'd let Morrison have the Prowler at cost plus ten percent. It had been in the yard for nearly a year. Morrison had a cashier's check. Morrison said he'd changed his mind and didn't want the Orca anyway. Said we'd gone over his head and installed

91

items he didn't want and hadn't ordered. Said he'd see us in court. Said sell him the Prowler or lose the whole deal.

But I knew none of it amounted to a hill of beans. The truth was I hadn't been able to stand my ground against the man and I'd ignored everything Jack had taught me. I'd let him make me talk, argue, defend, when all I'd had to do was smile, keep my mouth shut, and wait for Jack to get back.

I pushed myself away from the wall and suddenly I was talking. But the words coming out of my mouth weren't what I wanted to say and I didn't recognize the voice saying them. They were ugly, insulting, obscene. All of them specifically designed to belittle Jack's business practices and my place in his life. All of them lies. And when they came to an end, seemingly of their own volition, I walked out, slammed the door behind me, and drove away.

I drop suddenly to my knees, busy myself with a shoelace seeing Jack's just taken a game and they're changing ends. The tall guy – Austin, was it? – is stalking down the far side looking arrogant while Jack's taking his time, stopping at the net to towel off not twenty feet from where I'm crouching. I hear encouraging shouts from the onlookers, all of them aimed at the Austin guy, then someone near me says, 'Why can't the jerk get the lead out of his pants and play, for Christ's sake? He doesn't belong here anyway.'

I feel my hackles rise, I want to tackle whoever it was, flatten him, say, 'You're damn right he doesn't belong here. He's way too good for the likes of you. And what the hell business is it of yours how long he takes?'

And then it dawns on me Jack's playing a hostile crowd

here. That in all the time I've been watching, not one person has raised a voice in praise or encouragement for his superior play, and I'm amazed all over again that he'd be in this overly manicured playground playing such a pompous, poker-faced ass.

I see Jack, from the knees down, head for the baseline, then the sound of the ball going back and forth again, and I'm tempted to just barge out there, muscle my way into a front-row seat, raise my fist, and yell, 'Go for it, Jack. Get him. Show him how real champions play!'

But Jack deserves better than that from me. He deserves a string of apologies and the time and privacy to tell me to fuck off if he wants to, before I can hope to claim the privilege of a front-row seat in his life again.

Reluctantly I come upright knowing that although I'm ready to face Jack, take what's coming to me, this isn't the time or place.

I'll call first is what I'll do, I think, as I hurry away. Ask him if I can come over. If he says no and hangs up on me, I'll call again. And I'll keep on calling till I get to see him and try to put things straight between us, the past behind us.

I start to chuckle thinking how, once I get through the tough part, I can go on to the good stuff, tell him where I've been, what I've been doing.

'Listen,' I'll say, dropping my voice to a near whisper. 'Gonna tell you a story.' And I'll put my finger up to my lips and put on the face, the gloating kind of secretive face he used on us kids when he wanted us to settle down. And then I'll tell him how I got my act together and rattle off my achievements, my sales figures.

It'll take a while – I've been busy – and I'll tell him how with each one I'd mentally sent the news his way with the words 'Here's another one for you, Jack.'

No, I won't. I can't do that. Don't want to go mushy on him, have him thinking I've turned into some kind of sentimental fool. I'll just tell it all kind of casual, like, Yeah, no big deal. Because all I really want is to be around him again so I can start doing some of the giving and not just the taking like I did in the past when I was a self-centered kid thinking life was a one-way street.

ELEVEN

There are angry shouts as I come off the court after the first set. Hoots, catcalls, jeers, all of them coming from inside my own head.

'What in hell do you think you're doing, letting him take a set off you like that, Austin Sinclair?' one of the voices, the loudest, demands to know.

I ignore it, grab up a towel and bury my face in it. Then, thinking my action could be misconstrued, taken as a gesture of despair by Jack and the others, I lower it quickly and go to work mopping up my neck and arms instead.

'Six-one,' the voice rattles on. 'You lost six-one. And you call yourself a tennis player? Jesus! What are people going to think?'

I set aside the towel, take a long swallow of Gatorade, put on a smile, then turn to scan the faces that until now have just been a blur on the sidelines.

I see John Stewart, my regular Saturday morning doubles partner, sitting dejected-looking in the top row of the bleachers. He sees me looking and raises a fist, yells something I can't hear over the noise going on. Something that could have been 'Go get him . . . ' Or maybe it was 'Get your shit together . . . ' Either way, I agree with a wave of the hand and turn away.

'Hey, Austin,' someone close at hand says, and I turn to see Charley Snow, a VP from the bank, sitting with his wife. They're both smiling, but I don't like the way they're doing it. As though a smile is all they've got to cover the embarrassment I've put them through. I don't blame them. They stopped by after their own game to see me do my usual number, win, and to show by the remarks they feel free to toss around while I'm doing it what close friends we are, how down at the bank we're all just one big happy family. And now they don't know what to do. Stay and risk seeing me humiliated some more or leave and show a lack of faith. Tough decision for a guy up for promotion.

'Hey, Charley,' I say, shaking his hand, wanting him to know I won't hold it against him either way. I turn and wave Jack over.

'Come say hello to some friends of mine,' I say when he's close enough to hear. I introduce him to the Snows, then back off, leaving him to take over. I don't want to talk to the Snows or anyone else. Not until I've come to terms with the guy rampaging around in my head.

'So . . . what are you going to do?' he demands, kicking me behind the eyeballs. 'Shit, you weren't out there twenty-five minutes . . . Keep this up and you'll be home inside an hour!'

Like hell . . .

'Hey! You're the one who said he couldn't keep it up, but he did. Look at him! Does that look like a guy about to fold? Looks to me more like a guy who feels so good, he can hardly contain himself.'

He can't keep it up, trust me, I insist, watching Jack weave his spell around the onlookers, seeing them respond to his uncanny magnetism, their faces bemused, expectant, their laughter punctuating the anecdotes he's spinning one after another as deftly as he hits tennis balls.

'So . . . ' prods the voice. 'For no good reason I can see, you brought him here. Now how are you going to get rid of him? What's the game plan?'

The game plan, I say, my head turned towards Jack, my laughs coming with everyone else's, is the same as always. Wear him down. Wait him out. Play my game, not his.

I hear squawks of protest, things like mixing up my shots, coming into net more, changing my strategy, and I ignore them. I know I'm right. I think I hear a thud, like someone's slammed a door, and in the silence I state my case simply and clearly to myself the way I always do before I go into a meeting where I expect opposition, so I'll remember it well and not go getting tentative on myself.

One, I say on a deep breath, let's understand right now I'm winning this match. Me. Not him. Two, I'll wear him down so bad in this next set, I'll have him exactly where I want him in the third . . .

'You said there wasn't going to be a third!'

Enough! I roar silently while I'm laughing at Jack's punch line. Jesus! All this doubt. This worry. This nagging. If I wanted nagging, I could have stayed home and listened to Ellen . . .

'They're your friends, not mine,' she began, coming awake this morning at the feel of my erection hard against her buttocks and talking as though we hadn't just spent the last seven, eight hours sleeping. Talking, like she always does, so she won't have to acknowledge what I want while she scrambles to get her legs over the edge of the bed and the rest of herself upright.

That's Ellen for you. Holding her head high in my reflected glory. Playing to the hilt her role of Mrs Austin Sinclair, first lady of the town. Yet Ellen, in the privacy of her home, more particularly in the bedroom, refusing to be my wife at all.

'Twenty people is a lot of people,' she went on, her voice rising as she pulled on a robe. 'And why you expect me to stay here and wear myself out for them when you know my mother counts on me Saturdays to take her shopping is more than I can understand. Particularly when you're not willing to cancel your tennis to help me. And then you have the gall to expect me to loll around in bed all morning! Really, Austin, with you it's take, take, take, all the time. When will you start to give?'

'Come back to bed, honey,' I urged. 'It won't take long. Christ, I'm horny as hell. Look at me.' And I threw back the bedclothes so she could see just how ready I was.

She averted her eyes, tossed her head, and slammed into the bathroom.

'I don't see the problem,' I said, getting up and following her. 'They won't be here till seven tonight, and Jesus . . . you've got full-time help . . . a bartender coming in . . .'

'Help,' she sniffed, splashing her face with cold water.

'Help doesn't come equipped with brains, does it? You know as well as I do the kind of mess "help" makes without me there to oversee. And who's going to see to the last-minute details? Arrange the flowers? See that the grill gets lit. Do you suppose these things happen all by themselves?'

'I'll be home in plenty of time to light the grill,' I interrupted, taking her by the shoulders and trying to pull her close. 'And even if I'm not, the kids can help.'

'The kids,' she sneered. 'As if they'll even be up in time. They didn't get home till after five this morning. I know. I was awake all night listening for them. Worrying.'

That was a lie. She'd been sleeping soundly when I went up around midnight, but I didn't argue. I learned a long time ago not to argue with Ellen. Ellen crossed, especially over trivia, will disrupt the house for days, alternating tantrums with tears and long, stony silences.

'Make them help,' I said. 'Jesus Christ . . . '

'You make them help. They're your kids too.'

'All right. I will. Only please, come back to bed now. Just for a little while. A couple minutes . . . '

'I'm sorry, Austin, but I can't be all things to all people. You should have thought of this when you arranged your party behind my back and invited all those silly little bankers over. You should have thought about it last night.'

'I did. You had a headache, remember?'

'Yes . . . well, I still do.' She put her hand up to her head. 'I can feel it getting worse, too,' she said, tears filling her eyes. 'I think it's a migraine and you know what they do to me. I'll have to call and get my prescription renewed.'

Sniffing, she turned and left the room, wrenching the door shut behind her.

What happened? I wondered, watching my robe swinging from its hook on the back of the door. What in hell happened that a man and his wife never make love anymore?

Sighing, I sat on the edge of the tub, clasped my aching penis in my hand, and began the tedious, too familiar, business of masturbation. I reached for a towel to catch the semen, thought, No, Ellen might find it . . . guess what I've been doing . . . and reached for the Kleenex instead. I was just about to come when I thought, Why in hell should I give a damn what Ellen thinks, goddam bitch? What in hell does she think I am anyway? And I yanked a towel off the rack just as the first shudder racked me, doubled me over, wrenched a groan from somewhere deep inside.

I sat there a long time after my breathing came back to normal. I felt warm, drowsy, limp . . .

Sunlight, filtered by the branches and leaves of the great live oaks outside, poured through the skylight above me, making a dappled square around the solid shadow of myself on the tiled floor.

'You're really something else, Austin Sinclair,' I sneered, studying the slumped profile, the dangling hands, the lumpy outline of the towel still massed at my groin. 'A goddam bath towel where a woman ought to be. A straddled, laughing, eager woman nuzzling my throat. A woman with sure, deft hands fondling me, saying, "Come on sweetheart, please . . . just one more time . . . You feel so good . . . "'

Tears of rage, humiliation, self-pity, joined the sweat

100

trickling down my cheeks. Do such women exist? Do they? How would I know? All I've ever had all my life is bath towels. Bath towels and Ellen. Both limp. Both lifeless. But of the two, the towel's better. Towels aren't tight and reluctant and they don't pretend to be asleep when you're ready. Towels don't squirm with displeasure and tell you you're too slow and too heavy and too sweaty. And towels don't have heads full of rollers to scratch your face or breath that smells of stale booze.

Vowing, as I always do when I've just masturbated, to find myself a woman, a real woman, I flung aside my pitiful substitute and headed for the shower. But my imaginary woman, still insistent on my mind, came with me. I closed my eyes and felt her arms, wet and slick, go around my neck, felt her long, demanding body slide across mine. I put a hot, soapy hand around myself imagining that my heat was hers and once again, standing up this time, her legs encircling my hips, I was inside her.

A moment or two she lingered, my lusty friend, long enough for me to shrink back in size, and then she was gone; gone to wherever it is she goes when I'm surfeited, and I was alone looking at myself for what I really am: an old fart playing with himself in a steam-filled shower. A gutless wonder afraid to go out and make real what lives in his head.

Angry again, disgusted, ashamed, I turned and wrenched the faucet to cold.

So OK, I'm a coward. I admit it. But to me divorce is out of the question. Something I just can't face. I don't know how other men do it, where they find the courage. Or is it me with the courage, sticking it out? Still, how do they turn their backs and walk away from everything they've worked a lifetime to build? Their families. Their homes. Their image. And what if the next woman they choose doesn't work out? Is worse than the first? And then, what if, finding your ideal woman, she laughs at you? Finds you inept? Your inexperienced fumblings unbearable. What then?

I can't do it. Better to stay with what's known and safe. Learn to live around it as I have all these years and find pleasure in my work. My tennis. And leave romance and the expressions of love to other men. Men like Jack . . .

Feeling righteous, as though I had faced down the enemy for another little while, I shut off the shower and dried myself, shook out the towel, hung it up the way Ellen taught me years ago, and stooped to pick up the one I'd masturbated into. I bunched it up so the semen wouldn't show and shoved it in the laundry hamper. I've always done that, picked up after myself. Anything to keep Ellen happy. Off my case . . .

I gave the bathroom a final quick inspection, making sure I'd left it the way I'm supposed to, and was halfway out the door when the idiocy of the way I live hit me full force. With a savageness that appalled me, I turned back, snatched up the towel I'd so carefully hung, and threw it in a heap on the floor. I pulled the other one out of the hamper and flung it on top of the first. Still the room looked too neat. Like a model home with only a couple of towels out of place. With both hands then, I smeared the steam-fogged mirrors and it was all I could do not to slam my fists into the glass. And then I took my robe off the door and threw it in a heap on the floor. 'There, Ellen,' I said. 'That's how I like it.' And I grinned at my reflection in the mirror. 'And I'll tell you another thing, Ellen,' I said. 'I had it to do over, I'd make it with everything that wasn't nailed down before I'd choose a lifetime partner, and, honey, you wouldn't come close.'

A burst of laughter brings me back to the court and I see Jack miming out some story. A tennis story by the way he's waving his racquet around. A female tennis story from the way he's up on his toes. Let him keep going. I still have my strategy to work out. Where was I before the whole ugly Ellen scene got in the way? I believe I was about to state rule number three. Rule number three is all about trusting yourself. Believing in yourself enough to quit doubting the rightness of what you're about to do and doing it the only real way there is to do it, on instinct.

I forgot about that in the first set. I was too taken up with the strangeness of playing Jack again. Too busy watching for his old remembered techniques and registering the new. And I'd felt like I had to show him I was no slouch myself and so I'd thought about every stroke ahead of time, wanting to equal him in form, in power, in agility. And that's no way to play tennis. You can't play tennis and think about how you look and where you're going to go with very shot. Not at the level I'm at, you can't. At my level it's got to be automatic, spontaneous, and that's everything I wasn't.

I pick up my racquet, stuff balls in my pockets, and step out onto the court, promising myself this next set is going to be different. It's going to be mine. The novelty of Jack is long gone. And now I've got my head together, it doesn't matter a good goddam to me who's down the other end. Could be Sampras . . . Agassi . . . I wouldn't care. They're not the competition. The only competition I have, will ever have, is my own self and what I allow myself to think about, and I'm ready.

'Come on,' I call to Jack, so psyched I can hardly stand it. 'Let's get going. We've got two more sets to get in before noon.'

'You wish,' he says, interrupting some story he's telling to say it, then going on with the story. But as he talks and plays out his roles he's gathering up his stuff and moving out onto the court backwards, trailing a towel in one hand, a drink and his racquet in the other. I watch him stop to deliver the punch line, see ice cubes spewing every which way as he does so, and I'm forcing myself to stay calm.

Don't do it, I warn myself. Don't say it. You let him get to you now and you don't belong here at all. You're club champion, remember? Relax. A few more minutes aren't going to make any difference. Why waste good energy where it won't count?

He throws the last of the ice into the bushes and finally he's where he's supposed to be, at the baseline. I send him the balls and he argues it isn't his serve. Me and everyone else remind him it is, so he goes about the business of picking them up, doing all kinds of fancy soccer footwork along the way, and while I'm waiting I study the strings in my racquet and think about my last big win and some of the incredible shots I pulled to make it happen. And then I think about the deal I just closed at the bank, the one I could retire on today if I wanted to. And none of it's getting my mind off the sun that's scorching my skin. I feel like I'm standing too close to an open fire and I don't like it. We've got to get this show on the road. This kind of weather, with the temperatures up in the high nineties, the air still as a pond and heavy with humidity, can get to you, drain you, faster than any amount of tennis. But it's nice knowing it's beating down on him too. Nice thinking about all the energy he's throwing away on his bullshit routines.

I see him waving two balls, then one is aloft and we're back at it, first game of the second set and everyone please be seated.

Yes! Now, that feels more like it. That's how to return his serve. Just haul off and hit the damn thing. He can pack up his bag of aces now. He won't be pulling any more on me today. Didn't I say it was all in the mind? Damn right I did, and Christ, what a difference! Like night and day. Like walking across a room to turn on a light versus figuring out first which set of muscles to use and in what order and by what margin to navigate the furnishings in between. All things no human can do.

Playing like this, out of my own way, is like having a machine inside me, a flawless machine, and I do. It's the part of me that's looked on and registered all those hundreds of hours on the backboard, the thousands of hours play. It's the part that sits inside my head taking notes when I watch others play and when I sit in front of the tube yelling, 'Down the line, idiot,' or 'Crosscourt!' to the world's champions because, of course, from where I sit, the shots are obvious.

'All right!' comes a shout from the stands and a round of

applause for the overhead I just put away to give me the first game of the set.

I'm coming through now, by damn! Got the dial on the old machine set on 'Win' and letting it all happen. There's a feel of excitement in the air now and I feel generous, expansive, seeing people – the Snows – settling back relieved and happy that I'm coming through and giving them what I've taught them to expect.

TWELVE

Well, well, well . . . will you look at old Austin now! Playing like a kid out on a backcourt again. Only better! Playing like he's finally learned to get out of his own way. And in front of a crowd yet! The years have made a difference then.

Whompf! Man, there's power in his shots now. Accuracy too. He's splitting the tapes with them. Making me work. There's nothing I can send him that isn't coming back deep and solid and where I least expect it.

Like sparks, we are now, the two of us, reflecting off each other, bringing up our game. Saying, Here, take this . . . Aha! Didn't think I could still do that, did you? You ever seen anything like this before? Is it good enough for you? Will it shut you up? Make you go away?

'You're smoking now, Austin,' I yell. 'I'd about had enough of that "good shot" shit you were sending me earlier.'

And we thought we were good when we were kids! Man, we weren't anything compared to what we are now. We didn't have it in us. Didn't have the patience. Takes experience, living, self-knowledge, to play like we're playing now, and I can't get enough of it.

'Oh, baby,' I call again, sliding into a forehand and getting it back, 'send me more.'

Isn't this why I came? Why, in the tender, special hours of a weekend morning, I'd pulled away from my funny, incredible, lusty wife? Damn right it is. Course, there's that other matter too . . . God, but it burns me knowing that what I'm really doing here is begging. Me, the guy who stood alone since he was eighteen years old and thumbed his nose at the status-oriented Austins of the world.

Well . . . and didn't some old sage once say, 'The higher the bamboo, the lower it bends'?

So all right then, I'm bending. And if I creak with protest here and there in my descent, I'll smile and crack a joke, give them a show, pay my dues. And nobody but me need ever know what it's costing my pride.

What else is left to do? I've wheeled and dealed and sold and borrowed until right here, right now, is the only place left to go, and believe me, short of turning tail and running, taking off for Palm Beach or some other watering hole where the money's big and recessions only things you read about in the paper, that's bending.

But I'm doing it for others too, and that's what makes bearable the unbearable. I'm bending for my wife. My Jennie. And for her I'd lie down in the mud and crawl.

Two years I've been married to that woman, and still I don't believe the wonder of her. The magic. Two years and still I don't understand why a woman with her looks, her style, her humor, would want an old, semiliterate, debt-ridden hustler like me.

Women like Jennie, you only come across once or twice

108

in a lifetime, and unless you're stupid, you stay away. Hey! I've gone after my share of women in my time. More than my share by most people's standards. But I know class when I see it and I know myself, and a masochist, I'm not. I don't set myself up to get slapped down.

So it was her then, one bright Saturday morning, who left a women's foursome and came to ask me if I'd hit a few with her sometime, help her with her game.

Would I? Man, I was so charmed at being singled out from the guys I play with Saturdays – all of us standing around watching her, wondering who she was – I walked right into a bench and fell flat saying, 'Who? Me? Why, sure I will. Anytime . . . When? Now? Tomorrow? Next week?'

Five Saturdays we practiced together, her cool, detached, serious about her game, me hardly knowing what I'm saying for looking at her, wanting to grab her and run away with her. And all the time, in the leaden days between Saturdays, I was thinking about her. Dreaming about her. Telling myself to stay away from her. Then, contradicting myself, promising myself that next time I'd make a move and ask her out. And each week, when the time came, failing myself, preferring the certainty of knowing I'd see her the next week, even on so casual a basis, overhearing her say, 'Thanks, you're sweet, but my boyfriend and I . . . '

On the sixth Saturday, coming off the court, her going ahead, me holding the gate and staring at her legs, she turned and with that heart-stopping smile of hers said she felt like she owed me. Said her game had improved beyond belief and how about lunch?

'Sure,' I said, and started smiling, thinking of the faces on my buddies seeing us leave together. 'Only thing is, I'm a chauvinist. That means I'm paying,' I said.

'On no,' she said, a frown replacing the smile. 'It's my treat and I'm buying. Tell you what, to save your pride, we'll eat at my place. I'll whip us up some eggs or a salad or something.'

I followed behind her in my car to her apartment, though I could have led the way, so many times had I driven by late at night looking to see if her lights were on, sick with jealousy whether they were or they weren't. And while I was following her, I was warning myself to cool it. Telling myself not to jump to conclusions, that it wasn't me, just the tennis and her being the nice person she is. And I was reminding myself this was no ordinary woman and I'd better use every bit of patience I ever learned else find myself flat on my ass outside her door.

Once inside, sitting at the breakfast bar watching her set out plates, scramble eggs, put bread in the toaster, I had to swivel sideways on the barstool and babble anything that came into my head to keep my eyes and hands off those long golden legs, the swelling breasts – my mind off what all of it was doing to me.

'Why don't you open us a couple of beers,' she asked. 'Over there in the fridge.'

I felt myself turn red. Me, an adult, forty-six-year-old male, and I turned my face further still in to the room. 'Yeah,' I said. 'I will. In a minute. Hey, I like your stereo. It's a Sony, isn't it?'

I heard her stop stirring the eggs, felt her leave the stove to come lean against the bar. 'Is anything wrong?' she asked, and I turned to see her face inches from mine, her blue eyes clouded with concern. I looked away quickly.

'Course nothing's wrong,' I lied. 'What could be wrong? I just don't like drinking before I eat, that's all.'

She stepped back to take the eggs off the burner, then came around to my side of the counter.

'Would you mind standing up?' she said.

'Stand up? What for? I . . . uh . . . I can't. My back hurts. Must've pulled something back there.'

She smiled and in a move so unexpected, so bold I stopped breathing, she put her hand on my crotch. 'I'm flattered,' she murmured, feeling my erection tight inside my shorts. 'I'd given up on you ever seeing me as a woman. Now, will you stand up, please . . . '

Not taking my eyes off her face, afraid even then I'd do or say something that would spoil the miracle that was happening, I stood up and she was in my arms.

It was night when we ate lunch. Monday when I left. And in those hours of light and dark, of plunging thrust and moist heat, of muffled laughter and deep sleep, it seemed to me I'd known her before, somewhere beyond memory, and was only rediscovering what was already known, so familiar was her touch, her taste, her smell. And in the tender, drowsing moments between, I felt as though I'd come home from a lifetime of futile search and childish games.

She moved in with me the following week, cleaned up the shambles my life and house had become since the departure of wife number three, and then she made me marry her.

The woman of my dreams she is, the love of my life, but sometimes waking in life to find yourself living the dream is a heartbreaking torment. It is for me because my dream, the one I'd thought unattainable, became flesh and blood in my arms while the rest of my life was turning into a humiliating nightmare. A shambles of overdue bills and lawsuits, exhausted credit and foreclosures, all of it eating at my pride, turning me moody, undermining my confidence.

'Why didn't you come to me long ago, before all this happened?' I whisper into her hair late at night when sleep won't come.

She chuckles. 'You wouldn't have appreciated me,' she says, her lips and breath warm against my chest.

I groan and pull her closer. 'So much I want to do for you,' I sigh. 'So much I want to give.'

'You do, sweetheart,' she murmurs. 'You do. You make me happy. Do you know how unbelievable that is? What more could I possibly want?'

'A little M-O-N-E-Y might help,' I say, spelling it out. 'Enough to pay off these damn debts for starters. Then enough to cover you in diamonds.'

She waves an arm above our heads, and though it's dark and I can't see her hand, I know she's making an obscene gesture.

'That's what I think about diamonds,' she says.

'Why didn't you wait to come to me then?' I persist. 'That's the least you could have done. Waited until I got some of these kids out of college, some of these wives remarried, some of my property sold . . . until this goddam recession lets up and people start buying boats again. That's the very least you could have done.'

'And miss out on two years of making love to you?' she mocks. 'Are you crazy?'

'No . . . but seriously . . . '

'Shut up,' she orders, pulling away from me and reaching out to flick on the light. 'Now. Look at me. Read my lips.'

'I'd sooner read something else,' I say, reaching out to touch her breasts.

She ignores that and, her face close to mine, says, 'I love you.'

'You look like a goldfish mouthing at me like that.'

'Yes? Well, listen to the goldfish then. The goldfish loves you. That's the way we goldfish are. Loving. Caring. Sociable. Do you understand goldfish talk?'

I nod. My throat too full to speak.

'Well, guess what, then? This particular goldfish doesn't care too much about money right now because it happens to know that time takes care of everything. It knows that right around the bend in the river there's a pot of gold, time being the river, of course, in this particular fishy story. Now, tell me, do you know what time is?'

I nod, then shake my head. I don't have any idea what she's talking about. Only that it's her way of telling me how much she loves me and not to worry.

'Make up your mind,' she says. I shake my head.

'I didn't think you did. Well, if I told you they make watches so you can tell time, would that help?'

I nod.

'Good. Well then, if you watch a watch . . . Isn't that cute, watch a watch . . . Let's start over. Let's say if you watch a clock long enough, time passes. Agreed?'

I nod again.

'And as time passes, things change.' She stops to kiss away the words she sees forming on my lips and says, 'Don't argue. Just listen. Things do change, and they will. With time your kids graduate. Your wives, ugh – I hate talking about your wives – but anyway, the wives remarry. And next thing you know, this recession blows over and ta-da! Everything's back to normal again. Now tell me, isn't time a wonderful thing and aren't you a silly old silly worrying the way you do?'

'They might repossess my car,' I whisper, putting into words my worst fear, closing my eyes so she won't see the humiliation I feel at even admitting to such a thing.

'Yes? Well, you can use mine. You can have mine.'

'You need it yourself. And that's not the point. That's my car we're talking about.'

'Honestly, Jack,' she sighs. 'Where's your sense of democracy? Don't you know carpooling is the only way to travel these days? We'll share . . . '

I've got a million replies for her. All about my pride and the ego of the male and how I've always loved cars more than anything – almost anything – but I don't say any of it. Instead, I say, 'I love you.'

'You do?' she says, lying back down and holding out her arms. 'Then prove it,' she says. And I'm happy to oblige. Happy and proud.

So here I am, folks, I think, seeing people coming in from everywhere now, the way they do when word gets around a club that something special's going on. Here's old Jack – and only I can hear the creaks – come to show you a good time. Come to dazzle you with my tennis, my wit, my outrageous behavior. Come to trade you boats for dollars.

A few of them know me or remember me and they raise a hand. I can't hear them, but I know what they're saying. They're saying, 'Is that . . . ? Can it be . . . ? Is that old Jack Winston down there behind the sunglasses? The beard? Must be. Who but Jack would wear clothes like that? Run his mouth like that? Well, I'll be . . . '

The others, the ones I don't know, are saying, 'Who *is* that? A new member? Not in that outfit, he isn't. A friend of Austin's, maybe? Doesn't look the type. Must be someone visiting from out of town.'

'Have a seat,' I yell, while I'm diving for an overhead, hitting it long, cursing, begging God with outstretched arms to save me from myself. 'We ain't charging,' I reassure, seeing them hesitating, wondering if it's a private party. Wondering what's going on.

'Not yet, we're not,' Austin says, laughing, putting away a volley. And I'm thinking, I don't believe this! Old Austin's loose as a goose. Having himself a party, enjoying the crowd as much as me. Not that his fans are standing in their seats shouting obscenities like they would down at my end of town. No, no, no, and heaven forbid!

He's taking games off me now, too. That point he just won makes this his game and that makes the score three-love, his. And that's just fine with me. It's what I want. What I came for. Want to keep this crowd here as long as I can and as happy as I can so next time they hear my name, at the other end of a telephone, they'll know who I am.

I dangle my racquet from a limp wrist, pat the back of my head, and mince around picking up balls. 'Honestly, Austin,' I lisp, my voice as high as I can make it. 'I don't know whatever in the world's come over you. You didn't used to be such a mean, savage brute . . .'

THIRTEEN

When Austin called midweek canceling our regular Saturday morning doubles game for a match with Jack Winston, my eyebrows went up and I thought, This doesn't sound like the Austin I know. The Austin I know doesn't make hasty last-minute changes in his schedule. This is interesting. So I said, 'Go for it, Austin. I'll be at the club anyway. If I can't find a game, I'll come by and watch.'

'Thanks for understanding, John,' he said. 'I'll make it up to you.'

'Nothing to make up, Austin,' I said.

'Yes, well . . . I did make a commitment.'

'Forget it,' I said. 'See you.' And hung up thinking, Damn right I'll stop by and watch. With those two on the court, this'll be one for the books.

But now I'm sitting here watching them, I wish I hadn't come. Wish I'd stayed home. Wish I'd taken up the offer of the three ladies looking for a fourth Hal told me about earlier. Anything would be better than watching the two of them putting themselves through hell in the name of tennis.

I know the other people here think they're watching a fun, Saturday morning game of tennis. But I'm not fooled.

What I'm watching is two guys who've let their egos into the match so that, regardless of the score, both are losing badly.

I want to yell at them. Tell them to stop trying so hard. And I want to say, 'You don't have to impress us. We're already impressed speechless. You made your point years ago both on and off the court. We know who you are. When will you?'

I've known them both a long time and to my way of thinking, they're two of a kind, though I expect if they heard me say that, they'd call me a liar. Oh, I don't mean in appearances or lifestyle or anything obvious like that. What I'm saying is, they're two of the most decent, hardworking guys you'd ever want to meet who've worked like dogs to be the best in their field. But savvy as they are in what they do, they've still got a long way to go with their personal lives.

I came across Jack when I went out to buy my first boat. Had Julie, my wife, and the kids in tow, and we're oohing and aahing our way through a boatyard when this sharp-looking young kid in shorts and a faded shirt comes bounding our way with such an exuberant welcome, I wondered if he wasn't someone I was supposed to recognize. Someone whose family I'd built a house for, maybe?

'I know exactly what you're looking for,' he said. 'A boat, right?'

'Right, ' I said. 'Is there a salesman around? Someone who can help us out, answer a few questions?'

'Sure, but there's not a whole lot to it,' he said, deadpan. 'You put 'em in water and they float.'

'That easy, huh?' I said, watching my wife and kids dissolve in giggles. 'Great. But still . . . someone to talk to would be nice.'

'I can do better than talk,' he said. 'I can show.'

Oh, brother, I thought. Just what I need. A wiseass. But before I could argue, insist on seeing someone older, he had Julie and the kids wrapped around his little finger and all of us strapped into life jackets and out on the water.

I don't remember a lot of talking going on out there – boat motors at full bore are noisy things to talk over – don't remember telling him exactly what it was we were looking for: something small, easy to maintain, something we could fool around with on weekends. Just remember relaxing as his obvious skill and knowledge steered us through the clutter of small craft and water skiers close to land and took us out to deep water. That and being swept along by the sheer force of his personality.

Later, after we'd inspected every boat in the yard and were sitting across a desk from him, he'd shown the same skill overcoming my objections and steering us through the paperwork until I'd found myself happily signing for a boat twice the size and twice the cost of what we'd set out to buy.

'You'll have to come have dinner with us sometime,' Julie said as he walked us to our car.

'Can you come skiing with us?' our five-year-old daughter asked, reluctantly letting go of his hand.

'If you ever want to switch careers, look me up,' I said. 'I could use a guy like you.'

A Pied Piper is what Jack is. A collector of people. He can't help himself. To be around him is to feel special, and he has room for everyone. But that big, generous heart of his is going to be his downfall. I mean, how far can he stretch himself, both emotionally and financially, before he breaks? Like, when Jack divorces he won't sell the house and move the family into smaller quarters. That would only add to the hurt, both his and theirs. What Jack does is triple his workload so they can stay where they are while having me build another house for him. I've built two already and he was living in a showplace when I met him. But how in hell he's carrying all those mortgages, supporting the ex-wives, educating the kids, is beyond me. In the eighties maybe. But in times like these?

It's catching up with him, though. I don't have to ask how he's doing, he's showing me both in the way he looks and how he's playing right now. He looks overweight, drawn, exhausted. And he's in overkill. Trying too hard for the wit and charm that used to come so naturally and coming across instead as a caricature of himself, like an aging actor striving to play the kid role forever.

Austin's not doing much better. He's overplaying it too. Taking the serious athlete, club champion role to the point where he looks like a robot down there. Not that Austin's ever been what you'd call light or easygoing, but come on, let him save that stance for the office. Keep it for the overly ambitious kind of guy I was twenty-some years ago who went bustling into his newly opened branch office all primed to take out a big loan only to be told no. Man, that'll knock the wind out of your sails pretty fast.

We've laughed about that incident since, Austin and I, but at the time it was the end of the world for me and I wasn't laughing.

'No?' I'd spluttered, unable to believe my ears. 'What do you mean, no? Listen, son, I think you need to talk to someone higher up. They'll tell you I've been doing business with this bank since . . . well, you'd have still been in high school when I started out . . . and I've never been turned down. My reputation is flawless. I'm scheduled to break ground next month. I've got my subs lined up and ready to go. Here, give me the phone, let me talk to old Johnson. He's always approved my loans. He'll set you straight.' And while I was talking I was thinking, They must have lost their minds downtown making this kid a manager. Punk doesn't know shit.

'We can call Johnson now if you like,' Austin said, his face reddening. 'But the answer is still no. Your current subdivision isn't meeting projections to date and the economic indicators don't look promising for the next quarter. It's too high a risk. Hold off for another six months, fill up the houses you've got going, then we'll talk.' And he stood up, signaling the meeting was at an end.

I must have sat there a full five minutes, so outraged I couldn't speak, and I'd had to hold on to the arms of my chair not to reach across the desk and grab him by the throat. Finally, 'Think I'll just take a run down to your main office,' I said. 'Get this straightened out . . . '

Driving downtown, I'd nearly wrecked a couple of times going over the insult he'd just handed me. But by the time I parked I was over the worst of it and feeling almost sorry for him, knowing that by the end of the day he'd be out looking for a job. But he was young. He'd get over it. Find some other career where he could flourish. And next time around,

121

in whatever field, he'd do his homework, find out ahead of time just who he was dealing with.

Came to find out he had done his homework. I never did get that particular loan, and though at the time I cursed him and the bank to hell and back, he saved my butt that day. Interest rates went through the roof, housing starts dropped to all-time lows, and the guy who did grab that piece of land out from under me was in bankruptcy inside of six months.

I had a lot of pride to work through before I could bring myself to talk to Austin again, but the fact is, I wouldn't be sitting here today, financially secure, if he hadn't been there to keep me straight over the years.

But like I just said, I wish I wasn't here at all. It's getting harder by the minute to watch these two play out their self-assigned roles.

To tell you the truth, they're breaking my heart. They remind me too much of the way I was at their age and making my own life hell by living every second trying to be all things to all people. It took me a long time, years longer than it should have, to finally draw breath and ask myself why I thought I had to live that way. I mean, who was I trying to impress? What was driving me?

The answer was fear. Specifically, the fear of not living up to my own outrageous expectations. Expectations dreamed up by an unrealistic kid who had yet to take his first step in the real world. God Almighty, what an eye-opener! But there it was. Nobody was sitting around out there waiting to be impressed by me. How could they? They had their hands full impressing themselves.

What a waste of time! I mean, hadn't I already made every

mistake in the book and lived to tell about it? Worked my way through Acts of God and Acts of Congress? Set enough aside for a lifetime of rainy days? Sure I had.

So then if I wanted things to get better, what was going to have to change? Easy. I was. Was going to have to get back to the basics and do what I love to do – they tell me I was pushing dirt around, patting buildings into shape, in my sandbox – build houses. And let the rest of it go.

I'm not saying I've come to grips with all of it yet. I still push myself. But I'm getting better. Nowadays I don't climb the walls trying to force the whole world to see things my way, don't try to be everywhere or everyone at once, don't lose sleep if a project comes in late. Hey, shit happens! And I don't give a tennis match, or any other kind of social function, an importance it doesn't deserve like these two clowns.

I feel a rush of anger and pity sting the back of my eyes at the futility of what they're doing and I jump to my feet shaking my fist, yelling, 'Come on, you guys! Get your acts together. Grow up! It's about time!' And though I know they can't hear me over the shouts and yells of this growing crowd, I feel better and take off for the Pro Shop wondering if it's not too late for Hal to line me up with a game.

FOURTEEN

My God, but I'm having myself a time out here with Jack! Months, it's been, years, since I've had this much fun, felt so caught up in the moment, as though everything has come together and clicked. And it's not just me. It's everything. The day. The crowd. Him. All of it come together to make this one of those special times that blow up out of nowhere like a summer storm and just as quickly depart, leaving you ever after with a sense of wonder, saying, 'Do you remember the time . . . '

Too few of these moments I've had in my life, but enough to recognize one when it hits me in the face. And enough to know they can never be duplicated, only savored for the brief time they last.

Just hit the damn ball, I repeat to myself over and over. Never mind the hows or the wheres. Just hit it. And time and again I'm doing just that and I tell you, we've got some mighty pretty tennis going on here right now, both of us in high gear, going flat out on every point. And if the long silences during our rallies, the shouts and bursts of applause at the end of each, are anything to go by, then it's the best this club has ever seen, and it's tickling me to no end knowing I brought it all together.

Too bad I let my mother talk me out of making a career of this without at least giving it a whirl. This is where I'm alive, on a court, not in an office. This is what I am, an athlete, not a banker. No telling where I might have gone with it if I'd had my way. Could've been a household word by now. One of the greats. People nudging each other as I passed, saying, 'There he is! That's Austin Sinclair! You know . . . the only guy ever to win the Grand Slam five times . . .'

Course, I'd be retired by now, just playing the Masters to keep in shape and maybe doing a little commentating on the side. Chatting it up with the guys in the booth. All of us in matching blazers, the network logo in thread of gold on our breast pockets.

Or maybe I'd be running a prestigious tennis camp somewhere, grooming tomorrow's champions. Hell, why stop at one? You get a good thing going nowadays, you start a chain, right? Sell franchises coast to coast, my name and tennis meaning the same thing.

I must have been a pretty stupid kid, that's all I can say now. To have been free to make choices and not even known it. That's stupid, all right. Unimaginative too.

If I had it to do over, I wouldn't let anybody talk me out of anything. I'd go my own way and follow my own dreams. So maybe I would have starved, fallen flat on my face, but hey, I'd have been learning from my own mistakes and not from horror stories told by others. And I sure as hell wouldn't be living to regret steps not taken, avenues not explored, or thinking about what I threw my life away on instead: my parents' ambitions, not mine, Ellen's aspirations, not mine, this town, not the world.

There isn't a day goes by lately I don't wonder how this town would look to me now if I had gone away. Not necessarily to pursue tennis even, but just as the next step coming out of college. I mean, what if I'd taken off for New York with my degree instead of coming back here? Would it look ridiculously small and narrow to me now or would it still have the pull that brought me back in the first place?

The pull, other than the commitments I had – Ellen waiting to get married, my parents waiting to retire – was pride. Of course. What else? I grew up on the wrong side of this town. The poor side. And I'd needed to prove to myself my eligibility for its right side before moving on to other things. I'd wanted to feel I was 'in.' I wanted to see my name in the business section and the society column of its newspaper, not deliver it at dawn; belong to its yacht club and country clubs, not park cars for their members. And I'd wanted to own one of the old brick houses we have here. The ones set back from the street with sweeping lawns and old oaks on all their sides and apartments over the garages out back for the help. Jack bought one of those houses when I was still in college.

Anyway, in my youth and ignorance, I thought such a way of life the epitome of success, and with all the fervor of my ambitious heart I set out to achieve it for me and mine.

I was a busy man, believe me, making all that happen, and it wasn't until a year or so ago, when the last of my goals was achieved and I stepped back to admire my handiwork, that I began to doubt and question the validity of my goals. Get my name in the business section and the society column? For what? To see every remark I ever made twisted and misquoted? Belong to the yacht club? Why? To watch the town's senior citizens decrying the times we live in while they dribble in their soup?

Little by little then I began to taste the bitterness of ashes in my mouth. 'Now what?' I asked, and there was no answer. That long it took me to understand that everything I'd created now controlled me, that I'd spent the best years of my life building myself securely into a windowless, doorless box made up of petty pretensions and outmoded ideas that threaten to suffocate me now. And that's a hell of a feeling to wake up to at three in the morning, I tell you.

Oh, I've become a big man, all right. Don't doubt that. But I'm a big man in a very, very small pond, and I don't need to go away to see this town for what it is: a narrow, provincial little backwater fifty years behind the times. An ugly place laid out like a grid by the unimaginative forefathers of those I once looked up to with such awe.

Despite my best efforts, our downtown district is dead, all progress voted out by the narrow descendants of the narrow forefathers I just spoke about. Our merchants have gone away to thrive in the malls and strip stores that sprang up in the county, and all I have to flaunt my success to is a ghost town peopled by the derelicts that migrate our way when the weather turns cold up north. And in the meantime my best years are gone.

Jesus Christ, will you look at this shit tennis I'm playing! Where's that wonderful machine of yours now, huh, boy? Get a grip on yourself! He's not earning points off you,

you're handing them to him. You keep this up and you won't have to worry about the heat or any other damn thing. What you'll have to worry about is going home. To Ellen . . .

Yes . . . well . . . now, that's more like it. That's what they're sitting here expecting to see. Me hitting the damn ball. So hit the fucking thing then. And again. And again. And look at him sending them back, will you! Did you ever see such gets in your life? And I was going to play this whole thing on a backcourt! Make it a hurried, furtive event so I could banish him to the past where I thought he belonged! Shit, he no more belongs in the past than I do. We both belong right here where we are now. Where we should have been all along. Where we would have been if I hadn't been such an uptight, insecure prick afraid to include him in my calculated circle of friends for fear he'd offend those I so carefully fostered and undo all I had worked so hard to achieve.

I cringe now, squirm, remembering my despicable behavior when, newly appointed to Branch Manager, yet still feeling insecure, Ellen and I attended a party given by one of my newest and most important clients. Despite our hosts' unflagging efforts to get the party off the ground, it was a flat affair, the men all clustered around the bar in the den, the women drifting between kitchen and dining room, rearranging dishes, tweaking tablecloths. Then Jack and his then wife walked in and the air was instantly charged with energy, talk became loud and boisterous, the music went up, couples began dancing.

'Do you know that guy?' someone next to me asked, and turning, I saw Bill Jeffries, a fellow Branch Manager, but one of much longer standing than I. He was watching Jack whirl our hostess around the pool deck to a Beatles song while the rest of the party cheered and clapped in time to the music.

'Sort of . . . ' I said, not knowing which way the guy was going with his question.

Bill's mouth contorted into a sneer. 'He's a mouth on legs, if you ask me,' he said. 'Hasn't shut up since he walked in the door.'

'I noticed,' I said, only too happy to play Judas and agree with someone I deemed my superior. 'Well, we all know what they say about empty tin cans . . . '

'Nice of him to go out of his way to prove it, isn't it?' Bill said with a snicker, turning his back on the whole scene.

For the remainder of that evening, I never once made eye contact with Jack, never let on by so much as the lift of an eyebrow I knew he was present, preferring instead to exchange head-shaking, disapproving glances with my good friend Bill every time there was a roar of laughter from Jack's end of the room. Good old Bill who just might say nice things about me next time my name came up. My good buddy Bill who, within the year, was hauled off to jail for falsifying bank records. Jesus!

A thought suddenly strikes me that's so distasteful, I blow another shot, and while we're waiting for the next court to send the ball back I turn away and examine the shrubbery again. It occurs to me that while there isn't a person here who wouldn't miss their own mother's funeral if it were to coincide with an invitation from me, these people aren't my friends. Not one of them. I don't have any friends. And no wonder.

And then I see Jack, playing his heart out, giving it every-thing he's got, being himself, more real and more honest than any of these dime-a-dozen people I cultivated, and I'm thinking, There was your friend, jerk. Now tell me, who lost out, him or you? Ask yourself, do these handpicked, by-invitation-only members of your precious club find him loud and offensive? No, they do not. They think he's the greatest thing that ever walked out onto a court. And in the meantime, look at what you've missed. The laughs, the drinks, the tennis, the fun. And if you passed him up, how many others like him did you miss along the way?

But . . . where does a man find the time for friends when he sets out on his climb and he's working sixteen, eighteen hours a day and his kids have to go to private schools and wear braces and ride horses on English saddles and speak French? Didn't I say we have our pretensions here? Oh, indeed we do.

And how does he laugh it up with the boys, have a few drinks, when his wife's home crying because someone just bought a beach cottage and someone else is cruising the Greek islands and there's one big opening at the bank and four of us vying for it? It's contacts a man needs then. Contacts and money and hard, hard work. And friends just won't hack it.

Oh sure, we've got friends. People Ellen knows and approves of. Girls she grew up with mostly and their hus-bands, unhappy overachievers like myself. All of us long-married couples meeting every few weeks at the better restaurants around town to say the same things, crack the same jokes, as we did the time before. And to discuss with raised eyebrows and smug disapproval the latest scandals. The bankruptcies, the runaway kids, the divorces, the drugs . . .

Course, what we're really doing is patting ourselves on the back, just like my mother used to do, congratulating ourselves on our virtue, saying, 'Well . . . nobody ever said it would be easy, and Lord knows we've had our hard times, but what the hell. We stuck it out and now look at us. Aren't we wonderful?' Each of us talking louder and longer than the one who went before to quiet the unrest, the nagging suspicion that maybe the Cracker Jack we've been chewing through all our lives isn't going to be worth the prize at the bottom of the box; that what we held out for wasn't worth the price in boredom we've had to pay since.

So yes, I suppose I've got friends. But none I'd care to go drinking or carousing with – if I knew how to carouse, that is – and none to fill the empty, gaping holes of my life with.

I'd like to see Ellen get through just one day without her clique of friends. Jesus, no I wouldn't. Ellen without her girls to yak with, have lunch with, shop with, trade worn-out dirty jokes with, would be more Ellen than even I could live with.

Too bad she never liked Jack. Snubs him the few times we run into him socially. Too bad I didn't put my foot down and have him over anyway, had the kids meet him, get to know him. Too bad they're not here now, my kids. Might have done them good, opened their eyes, to see their dad in a situation like this, holding his own against such a character, instead of across a desk at the bank or coming in the door, whipped, at the end of a day.

131

Not that they're there at the end of a day anymore. Why would they be when they've got cars of their own and their mother's credit cards? What would they hang around for? To hear me ask them what they've been up to all day and groan when they tell me.

That makes me a monster, doesn't it? Ellen says it does. She says I'm a narrow-minded workaholic who has no idea how tough it is for kids today. She also says I'm an old-fashioned bore who doesn't understand about stress and peer pressure. (Ellen, Ellen, how do you think I got where I am today?) And God forbid that I should forget the ever-present threat of drugs or AIDS or nuclear disaster hanging over their innocent, good-looking heads. Or that they need space and time to find themselves. But Jesus Christ, is it really asking too much to expect big healthy kids to get up off their butts once in a while and do something? Anything!

Hit the ball, asshole, and cut this shit. Goddammit, too late! That's two games you've let him steal out from under you, and by God, they better be the last!

FIFTEEN

Something's bugging old Austin, the way he's suddenly let his game slide. His mind's way off somewhere. Somewhere he doesn't want to be, from the look of him.

'Come on, Austin, concentrate, will you?' I yell, seeing him flub another shot, send it long. 'You don't think I came clear across town to watch you screw up, do you? Show me some tennis . . . '

He snaps back from wherever he was and hits a backhand so deep down the line, there's no way I can get to it, though I fall flat on my face trying.

'That's more like it,' I say, picking myself up and making a production of spitting Har-Tru out of my mouth, brushing it off my clothes. And all the while I'm wondering what in hell can possibly be eating at a guy like Austin. I mean, damn, he's got it all, hasn't he? He's living The Dream, showing the rest of us the virtue of The American Work Ethic.

Man, I had it to do over, I'd hold off on the jeers, the laughter, till I at least tried it his way. I'm not saying I'd go as far as he has, be as drastic, but I'd sure as hell go in for a little more saving, a little more long-range planning, a few more investments. And I'd have believed in my dream woman too, held out for her, and not married every pretty face that caught my eye.

Not that I'm making a pitch here for Austin's personal life or that pretentious wife of his, saying he held out for her. Hell, no! That side of Austin, he can keep. The way I see it, Austin, for all his business savvy, is a coward when it comes to women. An emotional cripple. A guy who lets himself be dominated by them. I know that old mother of his pushed him around something fierce, and I don't doubt that barracuda Ellen has him snowed too, on some kind of guilt trip, else why would he still be with her?

Another thing I'd change if I had to do it over is my product. Think next time around, I'd go for something a little less luxurious and try for something a bit more practical. Something necessary like, say, bread? Maybe I wouldn't have had the fun I've had along the way, but I'd be willing to trade a few laughs for the knot I've carried in my gut these last couple years. The knot that makes me think I was maybe laughing in all the wrong places.

Looks like I got to old Austin back there. He's keeping me busy now. Too busy to even open my mouth and the score's climbed to forty-thirty, his.

That's how I need him to play. How he has to play. So I can keep my own head together. Keep it from straying away to pick over my troubles like some old derelict sifting through trash in a back alley.

'Come on, Austin,' I yell again, though he's playing great and it's myself I'm hassling. 'Let's go! Hustle . . .'

'Christ! How much further do I have to go?' he gasps. 'What do you want from me, blood?'

No, Austin, I don't want your blood. Just want you to pay attention. Want you to keep returning this yellow ball I'm hitting at you as hard and as often as you can. Want you to win this set so I can stay around awhile. But you've got to win it, Austin. I'm not giving it to you.

And if you don't – keep this ball coming, I mean – then I'm not going to be able to stay around at all. Not at this club and not in this town. I'm going to have to pack up and leave and . . . Jesus! Will you listen to me! Course I'm not leaving. I'm no quitter. And why would I leave? For a few lousy debts, when I've been in and out of debt all my life and laughed at it? This is my town. I'm comfortable here. Happy. It's where I belong. Where I grew up. The one place on earth I'm always thrilled to come back to. My family is here. My kids. God . . . my kids!

I feel the back of my eyes sting at the thought of living someplace where I couldn't see my kids, be around them weekends. And I start yelling at Austin again.

'For chrissakes, man, move it, will you? What are you, some kind of old grandmother?'

He looks at me strange and walks off the court. 'Are you hallucinating?' he asks. 'That was my point. That makes it my game. It's five-four mine.'

'I know it,' I say, acting like I do. 'Just keeping you honest is all. You know, alive . . . '

'Alive!' he splutters into his drink. 'It's you playing like the living dead.'

'That'll be the day,' I say, and turn away thinking, Wake

up, asshole! Tighten up! It's one thing to want to stay in the match, another to fall apart on yourself. Get sloppy. Give him what he ought to be earning. You let your mind run away with you now, baby, and you really will be dead as far as he and the rest of these people are concerned. You lose your concentration now, let your problems take over, and right away you'll turn yourself into an object of pity. And all they'll see you for is a badly dressed, no-class, loudmouthed joke, forgotten before you're out of the parking lot. You stay on top, in control, and you're a character, a guy who walks where angels fear to tread and lives to tell about it.

And now Austin's playing the kind of tennis they expect him to play, showing he can take care of himself, these people are feeling unneeded and they don't like it. They're on my side now. They want me to win. After all, they're thinking, he's won everything *so* many times. He's got the trophies and he's got the name. And the bank. And the mansion. And the money. So let him see how it feels to lose just once. To fail . . .

There isn't one of them that wouldn't like to be where I am right now. Cramming his almighty serves back down his throat. Calling him a lying son of a bitch when he calls a line against me. Fooling him with trick shots they never even dreamed about. They want to see him beat and they wish it was them doing it. Isn't that what people create idols for? So they can stand by and cheer when they're toppled.

I've felt the same attitude, seen the same look on the faces of the people that go to powerboat races. Car races, too. Rows and rows of weak, avaricious faces waiting, watching, to see if someone bigger, bolder than themselves won't hopefully push too far in an effort to achieve and maybe die over it. Sure justifies their own fear-ridden, fucked-up lives, doesn't it? Makes safe seem sane and not cowardly.

Too bad I need this win so badly myself, else, just this once – and as a first – I'd be inclined to let him take it. But this is one time I can't give anything away. I'm too damn close to the wire myself. Too like the rest of them here. And I need to prove myself otherwise because nobody knows better than me I can only get away with my style of behavior, a style as carefully thought out and executed as anything old Austin ever put together, if I come through with results.

I pick up my racquet and step back out onto the court. Whatever I am, whatever my problems, nobody's leaving here today taking me for a joke.

SIXTEEN

'Char-ley,' my wife, Susan, singsongs, nudging me. 'Oh, Charley Snow . . . '

Without taking my eyes off the point in play, I nudge her back to let her know I'm listening.

'What do you think?' she asks.

'About what?'

'About him.' And she gestures towards Jack.

'What about him?'

'Well . . . you know . . . I mean, look at him. He's not the kind of guy you'd expect to see playing Austin, is he? How do you think he knows him?'

I shrug. Shake my head. 'Haven't a clue,' I say. 'Austin didn't give me any more background than he gave you when he introduced us. Hush. Watch the match . . . Wow! What a serve!' And I'm on my feet clapping, yelling, 'Great point, Austin!'

But I'm wondering myself just who the guy is, Boston Marathon head to toe. Looks like a refugee from the public courts to me. Someone I'd expect to see subdued, intimidated even, in surroundings where he's clearly out of place. But he's not. He's swaggering around like he owns it. Not only that, but it looks to me like he's somehow got Austin off balance. Like . . . unsure of himself? I don't like it! It's disconcerting to see Austin behave in a way I often feel inside. Makes me wonder how I come across. And why would Austin be going tentative on himself when in all the years I've worked with him, I've never once seen him other than calm and unflappable over matters that mean a lot more than a game of tennis?

'He's adorable,' Susan says, chuckling over something Jack just did.

'Adorable?' I say in amazement.

'Yes.' And now she's laughing out loud, her eyes following him on the court. 'You know, like a nice, rough old teddy bear. He's fun!'

'Jeez . . . First Austin. Now you . . . '

'First Austin, now me, what?'

'You're . . . you're just not being yourselves today. Neither one of you . . . '

She looks puzzled, then jumps to her feet clapping over a particularly dazzling rally, and when she sits down again she gives me one of her wicked, knowing smiles and says, 'You know what? I think you're feeling threatened.'

'Goddammit, Susan . . . ' I splutter. 'I just said . . . '

'I know what you just said,' she says. 'And I also know you're sitting here all pissed off because this Jack person's come in here wearing all the wrong clothes, is playing with a shitty old racquet, saying all the wrong things, cussing up a storm . . . and Austin and I, and everyone else here from the look on their faces, is loving it. Face it, Charley. You're jealous.'

139

I know I've turned a dull red. I always do when I'm angry. But Jesus! I make one innocuous remark and Susan's all over me. And I know better than to sit here and defend myself now because Susan always speaks her mind loudly regardless of who's listening or what the occasion. So I shift slightly in my seat so I'm turned away from her and work at concentrating on the match.

But in my head I'm fiercely defending myself. And when we get home, she'll hear about it.

I mean, excuse me, but I feel threatened? I'm jealous? Threatened by what? Jealous of whom? She can't seriously mean that buffoon down there on the court, can she? What's so damn special about a guy turning his own first-class tennis into a clown's act when he'd be a lot more interesting – to me, anyway – if he just played it straight?

Must be me. Like the lady just said, everyone else here's loving it. Must be just one more example of me, the straight-laced New Englander, not getting this whole loud, good ol' boy, southern way of behavior where grown men run around acting like overgrown kids.

This dumb jerk reminds me of Bubba down at the bank. In fact, put Bubba in tennis clothes – all six foot four and three hundred pounds of him – give him a racquet, and you'd have the same results. Jesus, what a spectacle that would be! Let's all give praise and sing hallelujah that Bubba spends all his spare time on a golf course except in the fall when he takes his big slobbering hounds and goes to sit in a tree somewhere up in Georgia, 'huntin', boy. Huntin'.'

Bubba's work habits at age thirty-five are what mine were at age twenty-two when I was still young and naive enough to think that a degree was all I needed to live the good life. With an arrogance that makes today's me wince, I hightailed my way through a series of jobs thinking it ludicrous that I, a College Grad, be asked to spend eight hours a day at the copy machine, stay after five, come in on Saturdays, attend seminars. Shit! Where were the grunts?

'Looks like you've bounced around some, son,' Austin said, looking up from my resume the day he interviewed me.

'Yes, sir. I have.'

'Got a good reason for that?'

'Yes, I do, ' I said, sitting up straighter, readying myself to launch into my well-rehearsed litany of excuses. But then I'd looked across into Austin's stern, unwavering eyes and known he wouldn't buy the bullshit.

'Because I was a jerk, sir,' I said.

'Tell me about it,' he said, tilting back in his chair.

So I told him how unrealistic, juvenile, my expectations had been. How I'd thought I should start higher up the totem pole. I also told him – confessed – that in spite of my degree, I'd often felt inadequate and unprepared for the demands of various jobs and how more than once I'd quit because I'd been scared shitless of getting fired.

'What brought you south?' he asked.

'I had no other choice,' I said. 'Susan, my wife, was born here. Her family lives here. They paid our way down because she was pregnant. I . . . I couldn't find a job . . . ' And I nodded towards my resume lying on the table between us. 'You'll see my last position ended in 1987. I was a stockbroker.'

'Ah,' he said. 'The crash.'

'Yeah,' I said. 'The crash.'

'Have any of your own money in it?'

'Everything I could get my hands on,' I said, and tried to still my hands twisting under the table with an apparent life of their own, remembering how with rash promises I'd talked my dad into investing so I could meet my quota for the month and taken him down with me.

'You couldn't find another job up there?' Austin asked.

'No, sir. Seemed like everything fell apart at once. The job market. Real estate . . . '

'Did you lose your home?'

I nodded. 'And the cars. You know, the matching Beemers . . . '

'Humph,' he said, and swiveled in his chair to stare out the window.

In the silence I studied my bitten-down fingernails with frowning concentration, thinking, I've blown it. Why would he hire me? Shit, I wouldn't hire me. I mean, what a wimp coming across like that, bleeding my sorry life story. I should've stuck to the excuses. I had 'em down pat. Oh, Christ! How'm I ever going to face Susan, her family . . . tell them I blew it.

Finally Austin turned back to face me. 'Here at the bank,' he began, 'the road to the top is wide open. We're always starting up new ventures, new divisions, moving into new territories. There's room for dedicated people who have the right attitude, the determination. You could say we're like the Marines in that regard. We're looking for a few good men.'

He paused as though he'd lost his train of thought, or

142

was maybe rethinking that last corny line, and I'd wanted to jump up, shake him, say, 'Come on! Never mind the speeches. Tell me one way or the other. Am I in or out?'

Finally, 'Seems to me the world's already taught you the kind of dedication it takes to get up there. Stay there,' he said. 'You ready now for the long haul?'

I had a hard time not going down on my knees in gratitude, and he knew it. Without waiting for my reply, which he'd known would be long and stammered, he'd risen to his feet and at the door said, 'Be in my office tomorrow morning at seven.'

That was nine years ago and I haven't let up on myself once in all that time. Not that there aren't days, plenty of days, when I drive to work scowling thinking of the nonstop mountains of paperwork that land on my desk, the unfinished business waiting for my attention, and wishing I was the jet pilot or the mountain climber or any of the hundred other things I fantasized when I was a kid.

But then I get to the office and see Austin calmly going about the business of running his world smoothly and efficiently, making it all look so easy, and I forget my reluctance and think, Yes! This is what I want. That's how I want to be. I can do it! And I willingly slide into the role I'm working toward.

And when I do get there – to the top, I mean – I don't want some uncouth slob like this Jack person making me feel foolish about it. Because that's exactly what he's making Austin feel right now, a little bit foolish. As though he's holding up a mirror to him, and by inference me, saying, 'Take a good look. Here's what you are. You're a college-educated, very important banker. A perfect gentle-man. A leading citizen. But everything you've worked so hard to cultivate doesn't mean shit because take a look at me! I don't have to be anything. I just am. And who's winning all the games that life, and you, can throw my way? You tell me!'

Like hell, I think. Austin's not about to let you walk out of here a winner any more than I'm about to let Bubba beat me out of the promotion coming up. The one that'll make the winner Austin's right-hand man. And thinking that, I realize that maybe there was a grain of truth in what Susan said earlier about me feeling threatened because in spite of his pitiful work habits, Bubba has a good shot at beating me out.

'He brings in the business,' Austin'll mutter, frowning his way through Bubba's chaotic paperwork and sensing my disapproval. 'He gets them in the door. Gets their signa-tures on the dotted line. And he keeps them happy, coming back . . .'

He does. Bubba brings in more new business than the rest of us put together, and the clients love his back-slapping, loud-talking way of steering them through investments, his conversation laced with 'aint's' and 'darlin's' and 'you-alls.' Shit, they eat it up. Act like Bubba invented high finance.

He's got other good stuff going for him too. Things I can only hope to counteract with attention to detail and the kind of work habits I used to scoff at. Bubba's degree is in Accounting – Austin puts a lot of stock in that – mine is in Business Administration. He's got connections, an old family name. I'm the outsider, the Yankee. He's worked at the bank since graduation, and we all know my sorry background. And perhaps best of all – worst of all from where I stand – he knows how to push Austin's buttons, make him laugh, something I've never once achieved. Shit, the dumbass can even have me convulsed, holding my sides, when I've sworn I won't crack a smile. And you know something? I can understand Austin liking Bubba, treating him like a Most Favored Nation. If I didn't have him in my face all day, wasn't competing with him, I'd like the son of a bitch too. He's a trip.

I hear Susan laughing hysterically at my side, see the Jack guy returning a shot between his legs, his back to the court, and I want to say, You know I could be that guy in a heartbeat, Susan. There's no talent required. No hard work. No self-discipline. Any fool can be a bum. Oops! Sorry, I almost forgot. We need to make that an adorable bum, don't we? But we've been down that road once before, remember? And the road got pretty bumpy and steep after a while, and all the laughs and all the jokes didn't help at all, did they? So don't sit there telling me I'm jealous and I'm threatened. So what if I am? Don't you think I wouldn't love to be lighter, have the self-confidence to ham it up? You bet I would. But I've eaten enough crow to last a lifetime, dug myself out of one hole, and I don't intend to dig myself out of another trying to be what I'm not. Let the other guys win the popularity contests. I'm after the big stuff.

And now I've gotten myself so angry, so worked up, I just want to get her out of here so I can set her straight on a point or two.

'Come on,' I say. 'Let's go.'

'I'm not going anywhere,' she says. 'Look. Austin's just made two unforced errors. And I thought he was turning things around . . . '

Without even looking at the court where I've lost all knowledge of what's going on, I come to my feet yelling, 'Come on, Austin. Be yourself. Get him!' And sitting down, I continue to myself, 'And while you're at it, smash his face in for me, will you?'

SEVENTEEN

Well, I say to the person in my head, the one who likes to throw his weight around every chance he gets, did I have the measure of the man or not? That's my point, my game, and my set, and I did it my way. Through sheer tenacity. We're even now, and boy, but that shade, that chair, look good! Whuff!

Not that Jack didn't have his moments of brilliance out there. He did. Enough to make me dip into energy I'd just as soon have saved for later. Enough to take games off me. A few. But he had his lapses too. Bad ones, times when he looked like a little old lady lost in a supermarket, and that just goes to prove what I've said a million times: the winner of any match is the one who masters his own mind. So if I, down a set, and with all the shit I've got eating away at the old concentration, can take a set off him, a guy who already had a set and doesn't know the meaning of worry, then this next set, and the match, is mine.

I'm making a point of not looking his way, but the pounding I'm giving him is starting to show. He's not playing the crowd anymore. Is content to sit quiet in the shade and rest. Out of the corner of my eye I see him pour cold water on a towel and wrap it around his neck, gulp long swallows of Gatorade, both things I'd like to do but won't. I don't need all that liquid sloshing around inside of me and I don't need him knowing I'm feeling the heat as badly as he is. Maybe worse. Let him think otherwise. Let him think I play every day at noon.

I won't be first out on the court next time around either, because that's exactly what he'll be expecting to see: old Austin, flushed with triumph over the last set, hustling, chomping at the bit to get out there and drive home his advantage. And I'm not going to play it that way. I'm going to give him all the time he needs to bloat himself. Going to let him go out first to roast and fume while I find a million irritating ways to stall and keep him waiting.

The fact is I'm tired and I know it. I need every second I can get now, so when I do go back I'm ready to unleash the reserves I've been so carefully hoarding and finish him off with both barrels while I've got the strength left to do it. I'll be going for the lead right off this time and I won't put up with any more of his bullshit. And I won't take any more lapses from myself either. I'm going out there showing everybody what it is to stick to a game plan and bring in a win.

But for the next few minutes, make haste slowly is what I intend to do. Going to sit here quiet and breathe deep and let the feel of power I built up in the last set seep into every part of my being. To rush now would be fatal. Fatal and unnecessary. I need the rest and I've come to terms with the heat, know it can only become a burden if I let it, if I give it an importance it doesn't deserve. It's there. Period. And soon, sooner than he suspects, we'll be out of it altogether and then I can let up completely. Give myself up to the pleasure of my win and the good feelings that come from a hard workout. Then's the time to wallow in liquids, relive old times, let my mouth run as fast and furious as his does. Maybe I'll even tie one on . . .

'You've got a barbecue to go to,' reminds the part of my head that keeps me punctual, and I nearly choke, stifling the groan that rushes to my lips. Not tonight! Jesus, why tonight?

Thirty years it's been since I played Jack, and it has to be on the same day, the only day out of an entire year, we're entertaining.

Well, shit! But how could I have known I was going to run into Jack the day, three weeks ago, when I put my foot down and told Ellen I'd invited people in? I'd had it up to here with her that day. Months I'd been hinting about the hospitality we owe, asking her to please do something about reciprocating, and months she'd been putting me off. 'Later,' she said. 'Maybe in the winter when it's cooler.' Then, 'Not now! Maybe in the spring when it's warmer.'

When spring came, it was, 'Maybe in a month or so when I finish this new treatment the doctor's got me on. You know how dizzy it makes me feel . . . '

She blew it, though, the day, three weeks ago, when she said, 'Later. The house is looking so shabby.'

Shabby? Ellen lives in the most elaborate showplace this town has ever seen. She's surrounded herself with more linen and crystal and china and silver and paintings and antiques and bric-a-brac than they've got in the White

149

House! She buys and spends and collects and redecorates. And when she's through at one end she rips it all out and starts over at the other, and she tells me it's shabby! Lord God!

Can anyone wonder that I care to spend so little time there with her? Why I dread going home from here weekends more than I do from the office weeknights?

In the week, at least, I can call late afternoon meetings, string them out so long the only sensible thing to do, the only kind thing, vis-à-vis my long-suffering staff, is to suggest we wrap them up over drinks and dinner at one of my clubs. And if I can't find anyone – anything – to have a meeting about, God knows there's always enough unfinished business cluttering my desk to fill a briefcase and work on in my den at home.

But weekends! Weekends I doubt I'd draw a sober breath if I didn't have this club and my tennis to come to. This is my home, this club, not that overwaxed mausoleum of Ellen's. This is where I come to unwind, get away from things. Relax. Where I'm welcomed and treated like I count for something. Maybe that's why I pushed so hard for it then at the outset, though at the time I didn't realize what I was doing. Just thought I was doing the community a service and fulfilling a personal dream. But now I know I was desperate for a place, other than the office, where I could unwind without Ellen's nasal whine trailing me from room to room repeating the put-downs she delivered to everyone she came in contact with the preceding week. And expecting my undivided attention and approval of every futile one of them.

I'll never do it again, though. Invite people in, I mean. Not ever. This is the third year running I've had to go behind her back, and it's the last. That's it. Playing the heavy doesn't sit right with me, and the tantrums and sulks and insults I've had to listen to since I told her the invitations were in the mail are too high a price to pay for a few hours sociability. If entertaining upsets Ellen that much, then Ellen will never have to entertain again. I'll do it myself in restaurants. In clubs. Anywhere but in her shabby house.

But that doesn't help me today. It means if I stay around to enjoy myself, I'll have her calling me here, dripping icicles over the phone wanting to know what's keeping me. It means I'm going to have to go home and listen to her silence and fool with a lot of gadgets I know nothing about, while the hired help stands around trying not to laugh at my ineptitude.

I feel something jiggle the upturned sole of my shoe and look up to see Jack nudging it with one of his own. 'Come on, baby,' he's saying. 'Wake up! We've got a match to finish, remember?'

I scramble to my feet, horrified I could have drifted that far away when there's so much left to deal with right here: a tough match to finish. People sitting around watching, waiting . . . Jack. Christ! What's happening to me?

'Just giving you a chance to rest up,' I say, covering for myself as best I can. 'Letting you catch your breath. Don't want to send you home in a wheelchair.'

'Hope springs eternal,' he chuckles, walking away.

'Hey! Hold on a minute,' I say, striding to catch him up, playing for time while I grope to recapture the feel of the last

151

set, the attitude I need to take the next. 'Just give me a couple of seconds, OK? I . . . I thought I could last, but . . . I'm going to have to run to the john.'

He looks at me odd. Like he doesn't believe a word I'm saying. But he follows me back off the court.

'Ladies and gentlemen,' I hear him announce as I hurry away, 'our esteemed colleague regrets the delay. But it seems nature calls even the mighty.'

EIGHTEEN

If I wasn't seeing it with my own eyes, I wouldn't believe it. But I'm seeing it and I'm thinking, Austin! Austin! If you're going to start acting normal, forget your rules and regulations to the point where you'll leave a court – your precious stadium court, yet – in the middle of a match to go to the john, then what's to become of the rest of us? Who're we going to look to for the RIGHT WAY TO DO THINGS?

I'm laughing. Kind of . . . But there's a whole frigging set to get through yet, and the longer he keeps me standing around waiting, the less I'm going to be able to keep myself up for it.

Tell you one thing, though, looks like I better quit calling old Austin old. Austin isn't old. Old men don't take sets off me. Not when I'm giving it everything I've got, they don't.

It's quiet here now. Only sound I hear is the water sprinklers on the other courts *chunk, chunk, chunk*ing in one direction, skittering back the other, laying the dust for the afternoon crowd. Morning people are gone. Gone or here. Haven't seen a car go in or out of the lot since . . . since I don't know. Haven't been paying attention. Just know there's nothing moving anywhere. Too damn hot. Hot like only Florida can be hot this time of year. Hot and muggy and every stitch on me soaked through. Dripping. Clinging.

I pull off my sweatband, wring it out, put it back on. Swipe at my arms and legs with a towel to stop the aggravation of trickling sweat and they only feel worse. Towel's wetter'n I am.

It's blowing my mind all these people sitting out here cooking when they could be inside in the air. Or in a pool. Or out on the water in a boat I sold them, wet with spray . . .

'What time you got?' I ask the guy nearest me, a guy wearing a bandanna knotted at the corners to keep the sun off his bald head.

He shades his watch with his hand, squints at it. 'Half after,' he says, then adds, 'Twelve,' seeing me blank.

I grunt. 'Time sure flies when you're having fun, don't it?' I say, and drop into one of the chairs someone's brought out and set up either side of the net for Austin and me. I tilt my head back and close my eyes.

Two hours, I'm thinking, more, it took us to play two sets. Jesus, no wonder I'm beat. And I think, noon. It's gone noon. Only fools or kids would keep on playing this time of day in this kind of heat, and then suddenly, out of nowhere, the words of that *High Noon* song, a song that's tormented me since the day I married Jennie, are playing themselves with full orchestra in my head. 'Do not forsake me . . . ' they wail. And I'm looking at her face back of my eyelids, her beautiful, laughing face, and I'm cupping it in my hands saying, 'Don't you leave me too, baby! Not like all the others. Don't! Hang in there awhile longer so I can show you what life with me can really be like. Be there for me when I get home! Stay!'

I jump out of my chair so sudden, the guy with the bandanna on his head jumps up too, startled, like where's the fire, man?

I don't look at him direct, but I see him turning to his friends, his smile foolish, apologetic, his hands spread wide like, don't ask me, ask him . . .

I grab up my racquet, walk to the back fence where there's about six inches of shade, and lean into it. Jenny leaving me is one nightmare, daymare, all-time dread, I just can't deal with. Not now. Not ever. It's too devastating. But why would she stay? What can I offer her?

I push away from the fence and start pacing. Just what in hell is Austin trying to pull anyway? What's he doing in there? Bullshit, he's gone to the john. What's he think, I'm stupid or something? He'll be lucky if he needs a pot before this time tomorrow the way we're sweating.

So what's he doing then, taking a shower? Soaking his feet? Calling his broker? Listening while E. F. Hutton talks, then saying, 'Buy . . . '

Or is it Ellen he's talking to? 'Sorry, sweetie . . . I know I promised to be home for lunch, but things got out of hand here. I lost a set . . . Can't hardly believe it myself. Don't yell at me like that, Ellen, I don't like it. Ellen . . . !'

If not all that, then what? Gamesmanship? The old 'keep 'em waiting' routine? Pretty stupid, if it's that, seeing the roll he's on.

And what am I supposed to be doing out here while I'm waiting? Entertaining the folks? Sorry, folks, but I'm fresh out of funny words right now. Don't have a thing left to say to any of you, and if you want the truth, I'm tired. Sick-to-my-stomach tired of living behind this funny-man mask I created long ago when I was a kid wanting attention, and making noise, playing the clown, was the only way I found to make it happen.

I polished it good when I got into sales. Didn't have a choice. Wasn't anybody paying me too much attention, buying any boats, when I tried the SERIOUS YOUNG MAN approach in white pants and a navy blue blazer.

It's worn thin on me now, though, this act of mine. Turned sour. And I drag it on each morning with reluctance. Contempt even. Like a poor man pulling on an outdated suit of clothes. Wearing it because he doesn't have anything else to put on.

Oh, I'll wear it again. In a minute I will. And I'll go on wearing it as long as I have to get out of this crunch I'm in. But after that I don't see myself needing it anymore. Nowadays I don't need the whole world to notice me. Jennie's enough.

There's a burst of clapping, some shouted remarks – nothing crude, of course – and here comes Austin. He's changed his shirt to a pink one, and isn't that a shocker in this sea of white? But it's got a polo pony or some such on it – I can't see the details from here – and evidently that makes up for the color. Shows us Austin hasn't lost his mind. In it he looks fresh and cool and serenely confident.

I'm surprised there's no drum roll. Surprised he doesn't take a bow. But he doesn't pause, just strides along like

God, nodding here and there to what must rank as senior angels.

He sees my empty chair and his eyes rove the crowd looking for me. It's a while before he spots me leaning on the back fence in the patch of shade. I've crossed one leg over the other and my arms are across my racquet on my chest and he can see I'm pissed.

'Sorry about that,' he calls. 'Damn phone . . . '

He picks up his racquet and asks, 'How about new balls?' holding up the ones we've been playing with. 'These look pretty ragged to me.'

I nod, still not ready to be chatty, and one of the sitters, proud to do something – anything – for Austin, careens away to the Pro Shop.

'How about your shoelaces, Austin?' I call, still leaning on the fence.

Puzzled, he looks down at his shoes. 'What's the matter with them?' he asks.

'Maybe you can kill another ten minutes or so retying them,' I suggest, and I can feel the faces in the stands turn my way, frowning, like what's his problem?

'You don't think . . . ' he begins.

I push myself off the fence and walk towards him, torn between wanting to smash his face open for his presumption in taking off like that, leaving me with a head full of maggots and the words of a song I've busted radios not to hear, and knowing if there was ever a time and a place to keep my head, stay cool, this is it.

I know I'm looking belligerent walking towards him and I know every eye in the place is on me, but having said what

157

I just said, I don't know what to do about it, so I keep on walking, thinking, Let's see you get out of this one, jerk. Surprise me . . .

Lucky for me, the guy that went for new balls comes thudding back across the court and creates enough of a diversion for me to slide off the hook. Austin *pht-s-s-s* open the can, tests the balls for bounce, then hands them to me, all smiles. 'You want to take a few?' he asks. 'Hit a few . . . '

There's a collective sigh of relief at the way he's handling things. People are settling back, fanning themselves, knowing I'd have to be a real shit to take exception to what he's doing. No wonder the son of a bitch wears a white hat. He's come through the perfect gentleman again.

'Nope,' I say. 'Just want to get this show on the road and off the road as soon as I can. You ready?'

'I'm ready,' he says, 'and sorry about the delay.' And he goes bounding off to the baseline like all he's done all morning is peel a few grapes.

OK, I tell myself, while I'm waiting for him to get in position. This is where you pull out all the stops. Do what you say you're going to do and do it fast. You've got brand-new balls in your hand. Rip 'em out while they're still cool and fresh and blow him off the court. Grab the lead and keep running. Go all out on every point and don't throw anything away. And one other thing . . . Do us all a favor and control your head, OK? Keep it here on the court . . .

I put a ton of slice on my first couple serves, making sure the balls stay in on account of them being lighter, unweighted by fuzz and dust and humidity, and they bounce away over Austin's backhand where he can't get them back and everything starts falling into place the way I want: I'm winning the points and Austin's puffing. Good. Remember that. He's forty-eight. He's puffing. And it's ninety-something in the shade. Make him run . . .

I take the game. There's polite clapping and while we're changing ends I'm staying clear of Austin the way he stayed clear of me earlier. And I'm pumping myself. Psyching myself. Telling myself, You're on your way now, baby! Keep this up and in a little while you've got the match and the loan. All you got to do is stay out of your own way and let it happen . . .

NINETEEN

Jack the Giant Killer's back! A demon who's covering the court with a conviction and power that's no relative to the doddering old lady I was looking at in the last set. And, like an apology, I had to give him the added advantage of new balls! As though I was saying, 'Sorry I kept you waiting, old buddy. Don't be mad at me.' Which is exactly what I did!

Come on! That's Jack Winston down there! The guy who grabs everything that comes his way and runs with it, remember?

You better start remembering, boy! Start paying attention! Isn't the way he's playing now telling you something? You weren't so caught up being Mr Nice Guy, you'd see either he's got reserves you don't know about or else . . . or else he let you take that last set on purpose?

I don't want to believe that. Not that last part. He couldn't have been that cocky, could he? Against me? Try again, jerk. He could. Haven't I done the same thing myself a hundred times when I'm sure of who I'm playing and the score's been lopsided? Thought, Why bother when all I have to do is feed him enough to keep him worried, running ragged to stay in the match while I sit back and coast, save myself for the third. The pressure's all on him.

Not anymore, it isn't. Now it's on me. He's held serve, and so much for my early lead. Well, shit . . .

No matter. Knowing him, he'd have held serve if I'd given him old socks to play with, and I will too – hold serve, that is – if he ever gets through with his chest-pounding, hip-wiggling, aren't-I-wonderful routine.

I go through my usual big windup, only this time I put a little less muscle on the ball, thinking if his ears don't pick up the difference in sound, the lighter bounce will catch him off-guard and he'll slam it in the net. He does! Nearly puts himself in there with it too, and while he's struggling to keep upright, I'm thinking, Fuck you too, you presumptuous bastard! I don't need you giving me what I can take. And with the thought comes anger and I welcome it. Anger, controlled anger, takes me places I won't go alone. It pumps me. Refreshes me. Makes me feel as tireless and light on my feet as he so obviously is.

'Wide,' he calls on my next return, gesturing towards the sidelines with his thumb.

If that ball was wide, it was wide by its own fuzz, and that makes his call questionable, which means I'm guaranteed the next point no matter how I play it. I've never known it to fail. Either your opponent, thinking about, doubting, his own call, wondering if the spectators saw it as good, flubs his return. Or the court, with an uncanny justice all its own, gives him a bad bounce and flubs it for him. In this case, my return ticks the top of the net, teeters there a second, bringing us both lunging in, then rolls gently down his side without a bounce for him to get his racquet under. My point and what did I tell you?

I take him to forty-love and he fights me off. I wrong-foot him. I fake. I plot. I feint. And I can't shake him. There's nothing I can do to the son of a bitch he can't do right back. No trick in the book he isn't aware of, hasn't used and polished and won with himself, and God, but he's getting on my nerves.

I win the ad. He takes the deuce.

He wins the ad. I take the deuce.

There's no unforced errors from either of us now. No clowning around either. And no talking. Now it's just grunts and showers of sweat and the sound of our sneakers grating through the dried-out clay. It's one step forward, one back, for both of us. He wants to break my serve and increase his lead, and I'm damned if I'm going to let him. It's mine.

Everything in the world I ever wanted, he has. As though I've lived my whole life on the sidelines watching him help himself to what I had to earn or live without. So OK, I outdistanced him on the money. But what about the rest? What about all the other things out there I don't know how to earn or where to find?

Does he have any idea, him with his blatant self-confidence, what it's like to live without it? To deliberately assume, smooth on with the aftershave, an unsmiling, preoccupied mask so no one will ever get close enough to suspect the insecure, fearful being that, despite all the years, still lives just beneath the surface of this middle-aged man? A man who lives every minute terrified his so-called brilliance will be exposed and held up for fraud, as nothing more than a childlike ability to persevere where others give up?

As a kid, confidence was something I thought I'd acquire with maturity. I thought it would come with holding a job, marriage, children, the next promotion, the next merger. It never has. Nor has courage. The ability to act spontaneously, on gut, without endlessly weighing the consequences of my actions and their effects on others. Happiness never came either, though God knows I've spent fortunes trying to buy it.

And what about love? Where does he find it? How does he earn it?

In the eyes of everyone I know, my love is signified by the anniversaries piling up year after year. The anniversaries that say to the world, 'There stands a devoted, dedicated couple. And isn't it nice, in times like these, to see some people have solid, old-fashioned principles that stand the test of time, while everyone else treats promises like hasty, soon-forgotten, afterthoughts.'

To me those anniversaries pile up like dead leaves. Each one a monument to failure, to my inability to deal with the fact that my marriage is over. Dead.

And each year while the toasts are being drunk, the last-minute, hastily chosen, uncaring presents exchanged, I vow that in the coming year I will do what has to be done. See an attorney. Talk to the kids. Move out of the house. And each year, as I ponder the decisions to be made, the feelings of Ellen and the kids, the division of property, my own uncertainties about living alone, the attitude of my associates, I grow afraid. How could I live with the guilt? Function at all,

163

knowing how many lives I disrupted – maybe even destroyed – in order to satisfy my own selfish needs? And so I put it off, day after day, and try to be kinder, more understanding, more caring towards Ellen, hoping things will change. Get better . . .

And then another year trickles away and once again I'm drinking a bitter toast to my own hypocrisy.

There are other traits Jack has that I don't care about, enviable qualities all, but gifts from the gods as I see them, not things he's struggled to achieve. And by God, he's not taking this game or this match.

How many times have we gone to deuce now? Eight? Nine? Jesus! What do I have to do to snatch two lousy points?

Whatever it is, I appear to have done it. Over the applause in the bleachers, I hear a voice call, 'One-all.' And through the sweat streaming in my eyes, I see Hal seated in the umpire's chair.

'Nice of you to come out,' I call. 'How long you been there?'

'A while,' he says. 'Didn't call before because I didn't want to throw you. Say, what are you guys playing for anyway, blood?'

I shake my head. 'Would you believe, fun? Fun and old times.'

'They must have been some times!'

'What's the matter?' Jack calls from where he's leaning on the back fence in the shade. 'Don't you trust me?'

'Sure I do,' Hal calls back. 'Just got lonesome in there by myself, is all. No one around to talk to. Everyone's out here.'

I'd give a lot for this to be an odd game, not an even. My throat's so dry I can hardly swallow, while the rest of me, everything I've got on, is soaked through. If that was anyone else down there, I'd let it go. Say, 'It was fun, sport, but . . . enough's enough! We'll finish it up some other time . . . '

I can just hear him if I did too. 'What's that, boy?' he'd holler, piling on the southern. 'Heat getting to you, you say? Bullshit! More like it's my tennis! My tennis and old age!'

And even though the words are in my head, not on his lips, they make me so damn mad I can hardly see straight, and I think, Boy, if you can keep this up, then you better believe I can too!

And then I'm warning myself again not to let him get to me. Reminding myself that that will only hurt me, not him. And that I'm looking at another chance to break him right now, and that pretty soon I'm going to have myself a nice win to store away in the back of my mind for a rainy day.

TWENTY

Would someone please tell me how come I let Austin hold serve when this whole set was supposed to be an exercise in blitzing him off the court? Time after time I had the ad, one point away from game, and each time I let him take it back. Shit! It's getting so deuce is the dirtiest word I ever heard.

I can't get anything past him. Doesn't matter where I put the ball, what kind of spin I use, how I fake or disguise, he's there ahead of me, his long legs covering the court like it's no bigger than a closet, reading my mind. Giving me the creeps.

Just what kind of player has he turned into anyway, playing so loose, so detached? Like I'm some kind of kid needing to be taught a lesson. Son of a bitch isn't hardly sweating either. Why would he? He's not carrying twenty pounds of flab and the remains of last night's six-pack in his gut, is he? Not our Austin. I suspect our Austin dined early on wheat germ and bean sprouts and had himself in bed at nine, celibate. If he runs his wide and wonderful world of finance the way he's running this court, then no wonder he's so damn successful. Christ! You'd be defenseless sitting across a desk from him. Swallowed alive!

I hear a burst of applause as he racks up his first point in this game.

'Thirty-fifteen,' Hal calls from the chair, and I whack my racquet against my thigh, punishing myself for letting him into the game at all, reminding myself I'm not here to glorify Austin Sinclair. Let his buddies here do that for him. I'm here to play this point. And then the next one. And then the one after that. And that's all. Haven't I been around this game, this world, long enough to know it's not him that'll beat me but what I think of him that'll do me in, undermine me, if I let it? Start thinking he's some kind of Superman down there, start seeing him as something more than he is, and I might as well hang it up right now. For my purposes that's just a body down there. Something that returns balls. Period.

I head for the back fence to pick up balls and I take my time doing it, fumbling them between foot and racquet way longer than I need to. Fact is, there's balls up there at the net closer than these here, but I tell you, this heat's getting to me so bad I can hardly stand it, and I need shade like a dying man needs a priest. Feels like my skin's not there anymore. Feels like I'm all over raw, smoldering meat. Austin may be used to playing this time of day, but not me!

If this was any other day, any other place, any other person, I'd say enough already! Let's go have a beer. But it's not and I won't. Goddammit, I can't!

I throw the ball up to serve, then let it bounce. The sun's directly overhead and I can't see a thing. Can't hit what you can't see, can you? And that makes me think I ought to be lobbing him more. Blinding him. Filling his eyes up with big black dots.

I toss again, not thinking about the sun anymore but about how serving came as natural to me as breathing. And how you can, too, hit what you can't see if you just let it flow. And pretty soon, lobbing every chance I get, the score's forty-fifteen, mine, and I'm thinking, one more point, baby! Just one more and you're wallowing in shade like a hog in mud.

Austin thinks different, and God, but his tenacity is a torturous, wearisome thing. Before I know what's happened, he's fought his way up there beside me and Hal's calling deuce again. So what am I going to do, hang around out here bitching about the heat and the sun ten, fifteen more minutes on my own serve?

Seems like that's exactly what I'm going to do. He forces me to deuce twice more before I pull it out, and none too soon. Somewhere along in there I pulled something in my shoulder. It's not much. Nothing Austin need know about, zero in on, but I'll be happy to let up on it while he serves.

Someone's brought out a stack of fresh towels and jugs of iced Gatorade, dripping moisture, and it's all I can do not to dump one over my head. I drink it instead, all in one swallow, then pick up a towel and it's cool and smells good and feels like the first dry thing I ever held in my life. I bury my face in it.

I sit down thinking how it's the little things that count when you get down to basics. I mean, just having the weight off my feet right now feels so luxurious, I'm surprised they don't charge for the pleasure. But even while I'm loving it,

I'm getting back up again. I'm too pumped to stay put. It's two-one mine and I want to get back out there, finish this thing up, put us both out of our misery before I'm too seduced by comfort to ever move again. Anyway, this match isn't the end of the road for me. There's still that other matter to deal with before I can let up on myself.

'Come on, Austin,' I yell over the babble of voices. 'Time's up. Let's go!'

He looks at his watch. 'What's your hurry?' he asks. 'We've got all day.'

Maybe he does. I don't. I sit around out here much longer, that door in my head'll start creaking open again. The door concealing the minus dollar signs. Jennie leaving. My car on the back of a wrecker . . . I can't let that happen.

Over on the next court I see the sprinklers still going. Four jets of water arcing over the court, one from each corner, and I don't stop to think. Just feel myself moving towards them, jumping a knee-high hedge . . . and then I'm at their center. Not getting any wetter than I already am. Only cooler . . .

The eyes following me as I trot back are round. That's all. Just round. The faces they belong to haven't turned away from me long enough yet to consult with one another and decide if what I just did was outrageously funny or outrageously uncouth. Don't know myself. Just know it felt good while it lasted and hey! If Austin can go off change shirts like he did, then I can take public showers.

I'm sorry for Austin, though. I can see from the way he's standing, face blank, I've embarrassed him speechless. He no

169

more knows whether to laugh or cry than the rest of them, and they're looking to him for a clue.

'Feel any better?' he asks finally, not going one way or the other but right down the middle.

'Yeah,' I say, toweling off. 'Lots. You ought to try it. Can we play now or is there time for another quick splash?'

'We'll play!' he says, grabbing up his racquet quick, and I'm following him out to that pitiless heat again, my shoes squishing every step of the way.

I see Hal climbing back up in his chair, and then four kids, one of them about my youngest son's age, come out and station themselves, two at the net and one at each end of the court.

'You mean we get to have ball boys?' I say to the one my son's age.

'Yes, sir,' he says, his voice young, unbroken.

I want to hug him. 'That's good,' I tell him, wishing he was one of mine. Wishing I could go on fathering kids till I was too old to get it up anymore. 'You stick around and watch close,' I go on, 'and I'll show you ways to beat old Uncle Austin you've never even dreamed about.'

TWENTY-ONE

'Are they, like, done yet?' Todd asks, opening one eye at a loud burst of applause.

'Not yet,' I say. 'They're at deuce again.'

'Shit . . . ' he groans. 'They keep it up with their ads and their deuces much longer, I'll be, like, an old man before we get out of here.' And he closes his eye, folds his arms across his chest, and squirms to get more comfortable on the hot, sticky plastic seat next to me in the golf cart.

'The stadium court match'll be over in fifteen, twenty minutes,' Hal had said, looking at his watch. 'And I need you kids to stick around and do maintenance on it before you take off. I'm shorthanded today.' And he'd hurried away, clipboard in one hand, cellular phone in the other, only to turn back and say, 'The boom box stays in the locker room, Todd, OK? And don't park any closer to that court than . . . Just park under that tree at the north end. You know the one I mean. And keep it down, both of you. Austin Sinclair's on that court.'

That was forty-five minutes ago.

I look sideways at Todd, who's still dozing, and wonder how come he's made me feel like I'm the new kid all day when it's him that's only worked here a week. Like, just for starters, how come he's been the one in the driver's seat of the golf cart all morning?

Course, I'm only allowed to work weekend mornings on account of school, and from what he's been saying, I guess he's working here nights, too. Even though he is the same age as me. Sixteen. But, like, everyone knows public school's a piece of cake compared to the private school I go to.

'I'm gonna go sweet-talk that old drone in the Snack Bar into giving me a free drink,' he says, coming upright suddenly, like someone just poked him.

'But Hal said to wait here till the match is over . . . '

'Screw Hal,' he says, flipping on the cart switch.

Somehow I manage to get myself out of the cart before he hits the peddle and goes crashing off to the Snack Bar, sideswiping every bush and flower bed he passes on the way.

He's going to get it, I think, seeing Hal look up from his seat in the umpire's chair, his eyes following the cart's zigzag path towards the Snack Bar, the court brooms attached to the back bouncing crazily every which way. I hope he gets it. Dumb jerk. He's gotta be the only person here doesn't know to stay put when the ball's in play so you don't distract the players.

With nothing left to sit on anymore, I lean against the tree and secretly wish I'd had the guts to defy Hal and go get me a drink too. Then I remember gloomily that even if I did defy Hal, I don't have any money on me anyway and I know there's no way in the world Todd's going to sweet-talk anyone into giving him a free drink, so he's wasting his time.

Damn! Here he comes back again, steering even more crazily than before because now one hand's holding the biggest-size drink the club sells, and even from here I can see it's not water.

'What'd I tell you?' he hollers when he's right opposite the stadium court where everyone can hear him. 'The old loon caved in . . . '

Oh, man . . . I hope he really gets it, I think, trying to look as though he's not calling out to me in case Hal thinks I'm in on this with him. Like, I hope they fire him. Probably will, too, just as soon's this match is over. And good riddance. He makes me feel, like . . . I don't know . . . like everything I say . . . do . . . is stupid somehow. Not cool. Like he's got an edge.

'Are they about done now?' he asks at the end of a huge gulp that leaves trickles running down the faint stubble on his chin.

'I . . . I don't know,' I say. 'I lost track of the score.'

'Maybe it's because they're so old,' he says thoughtfully after watching the players for a minute or two.

'So old?' I say, not understanding his meaning.

'Yeah. You know. Like maybe they're slower. Like, wouldn't younger guys get done sooner?'

'Tennis isn't like that,' I begin, and then I realize. 'You don't know how to play, do you?' I say, feeling all at once superior, like maybe I do have an edge.

He shrugs. 'What's to know?' he asks. 'Like, what's to hitting a little ball with a bat the size of a barn door? My

173

two-year-old brother can do that. Course I know how to play.'

I can't help laughing even though I don't want him to think he's some kind of wit. A comedian. But, like, a bat? This kid doesn't know shit.

'There's more to it than that,' I say, eager to impart a little knowledge. 'Like, there's a lot of skill in where you hit the ball. The angles. The spin you use. How you can fool your opponent. And, like, there's rules . . . '

He rolls his eyes. 'OK, OK,' he says. 'I got it! Like you gotta be a genius to get the ball over the net and inside that big square! So how good are you?'

'Well . . . I . . . ' I begin thinking of all the hours I've spent in clinics and on the backboard trying to zing in winners and look like Hal, and I'm about to say, no, I'm really not that good. But then I think, if he can't play at all, I'd probably look pretty good to him, so I decide to lie and say, 'I oughta be. I've been playing since I was, like, four years old. You want me to teach you? I could ask Hal to let us have a court in the off-hours . . . '

'Are you, like, nuts?' he says. 'Waste my time hitting a ball around like them?' And he squints over to where Austin and the other guy are lunging and grunting round the court, their faces bright red, sweat showering every which way. 'You'd, like, have to be crazy. Out of your fucking mind, crazy. Jesus! Run around chasing a ball in this kind of heat? Even a little kid wouldn't be that stupid. And they're, like, grown men. Supposed to be, anyway. Except they're not. What they are is . . . is . . . ' And he shrugs like he can't even find words to express his disgust.

And seeing them from his ignorant point of view, I got to agree they do look pretty retarded running around like that. Only I know they're not. Know it's him, Todd, that doesn't get it. Doesn't understand the good feeling you get when you serve an ace, zing in a winner.

And I've got to admit – though I'd kill before I'd let him know – that I really don't like tennis at all. In fact, I hate it. Like I hate all sports. All that running. All that chasing. Coaches yelling at you. Parents yelling at you. And for what? Nothing I've ever been able to figure out. I mean when the game's over, what have you got? Nothing I can see. I mean, it's not like you're making music and you can record it. Keep it. Play it back. Work on making it better . . .

That's what I'd really like to do, what I've wanted to do since as far back as I can remember, learn to play an instrument. I don't even care which one. Just so I could be part of putting all those notes and all those instruments together and making it all come out just the way I want.

'Don't be ridiculous,' my mom always says when I tell her I'd like to hang up my racquet and pick up an instrument. 'You don't have to be a pro, but tennis is a great social asset, a passport. A good player can get into the most exclusive clubs in the world, no questions asked. And it'll keep you in shape. You'll thank me one day.'

'I know he looks it right now, but, like, Austin's not stupid,' I tell Todd. 'How could he be? He's a millionaire.'

But Todd's not listening, he's pacing. 'I've gotta get out of here,' he fumes, looking at his watch. 'Like, I've got more important things to do than wait around on these old farts to kill themselves. I've got my life, my band, waiting

on me. Like, the deal was six to twelve on weekends. That's
what Hal said. And we shook on it. And, like, there's child
labor laws, you know. Hey! I got it. I'll hit him up for
overtime.'

But now it's me not listening. 'You've got a band?' I inter-
rupt, trying not to sound too awed.

'Course I got a band,' he says, like, doesn't everybody.

I stare at him, my head so full of questions, I don't
know which one to ask first, like, 'Where do you . . . ?
What . . . ? How long have you . . . ? Do you . . . ?' Finally
I manage to get one out. 'Like . . . what instrument do you
play?'

'Guitar,' he says, and instantly he's whirling and stomping
around playing an air guitar. 'Couple more years,' he says,
'and I'll be, like, the biggest rock star this country, this
planet, has ever known.'

'Don't you need to be able to, like, sing to be a rock star?'
I ask, listening to the weird kind of *dum-dum*ming sound
he's making to accompany his silent guitar.

'Like, what's singing got to do with it?' he snorts. 'None
of them guys can sing. What you gotta be, man, is, like,
cool. And I am. I am one cool dude. Here . . . ' And he
stops his performance. 'You got a piece of paper on you?
A pen?'

I stare at him blank while I grope in my shorts pocket and
pull out a soggy wad of paper with my mother's handwriting
on it. It's a list of stuff I'm supposed to pick up at the store
on my way home.

'Give it here,' he says, and snatches both the paper and the
ballpoint I've unclipped from my key chain.

Smoothing out the paper, he puts it on the seat of the golf cart and writes, then hands it to me.

'"Good luck to my oldest friend, Richard,"' I read out loud. And then there's an illegible squiggle and then, real big, the printed words 'THE BLEEDING SCABS.'

'Hang on to that,' he says, grinning. 'Frame it. Like, a couple years from now, man, it'll be worth millions.'

'God, thanks!' I say, carried away by the certainty of his vision, believing him. And I carefully fold the shopping list. 'But, like . . . won't it take longer than two years? I mean, like, you gotta finish school and . . . '

He looks at me pityingly. 'Like, how old was Elvis when he made it? And Bruce, baby? The Beatles? Shit, man, Michael Jackson was a fucking billionaire when he was, like, five years old!'

'Yeah . . . ' I breathe, remembering. 'Right . . . '

'The tall, skinny one out there's Austin, right?' he says, changing the subject so fast, it takes me a minute to come back to where we're at.

'Yeah,' I say. 'The tall skinny one.'

'And, like, he's a millionaire?'

'Yeah,' I say, glad to know something he doesn't. 'He's—'

'Maybe,' Todd interrupts, his eyes narrowing, 'just maybe, I'll, like, let him be the one to give me my first big break . . . '

'Why don't you ask him?' I say, hoping I'll be there to check out Austin's face if he does. I mean, I don't even need to hear his music to know it's gotta be pure shit. So what makes him think Austin'll even listen?

177

'I'm gonna,' he says. 'Gonna ask him if we can, like, do a gig here next big function they have. He'll be stoked. Oughta be. And then when that's over and he's, like, thanking me, begging me to come back next month and do it again, that's when I'll hit him up for a loan so we can get some wheels – like, maybe a bus – get our show on the road.' And his eyes glaze over as he stares toward the future.

'Couple of years from now,' he goes on, 'when me and the band are at the top of the charts, on MTV twenty-four hours a day, I'll, like, go out of my way to come back. I'll get out of my limo and I'll go, "Austin, my man, you were there at the beginning. You helped us out. And to show you the kind of guy I am, I'm gonna put this little club of yours on the map. Gonna throw you a party. Give you a free gig." And his eyes'll, like, mist up, and he'll go, "You'd do that for me? When you get paid a million bucks a show!" And I'll go, "Think nothing of it, man. Like hey, that's just the way I am."'

I hear Todd give a big satisfied sigh and then I hear him chewing ice cubes, swishing the ones that are left around in the bottom of the cup. And I open my eyes and see he's climbing back into the golf cart.

'You going someplace?' I ask, seeing him reach for the switch.

'I'm getting the hell out of here,' he says, backing up.

'But . . . like, where you . . . ?'

'I already told you I got business to attend to. My band's waiting on me. We got a new number to rehearse. Like, we got a gig tonight, man. And I'm getting out of this frigging heat and into some AC. Tell Hal I quit. Tell him I'll be back for my check. And tell him he owes me overtime.'

'But, like . . . your gig for Austin,' I say. 'Your loan . . . '

He pauses, looks over to where Austin and the other guy are still tottering around the court, and waves his hand in dismissal. 'I'll be in Hollywood before they get off that court the way they're going,' he says. 'The guy's a moron even if he is worth millions. Plenty more like him around. It's his loss, not mine. Like, he had his chance and he blew it.'

And before I can think to tell him to leave me the golf cart, that I'll need it to brush the court, he's cruising away towards the parking lot. And I'm left standing like a dork waiting to clean up a court these guys are trashing worse than anything I ever saw.

'Yeah . . . ' I mutter. 'Like, in your dreams you'll be a rock star. On MTV. You dumb jerk.' And then I think, like, what do I know? Maybe he will. He sure had me going there for a while. And, like, he did sweet-talk them out of a free Coke. A big one, too.

I'd still sooner be an Austin kind of guy, I think defiantly, trying to drown out the doubts the jerk has put in my head. I really would. And warming to my future, the one my parents have been telling me about all my life, I think, Yeah . . . and, like, when that loser's been laughed out of every recording studio in the country – the world – it'll be me sitting behind a big, shiny desk, my degrees hanging in matching frames all around the room. And it'll be him coming crawling to me for a loan, a handout, anything he can get. And, like, man, will I ever make him beg. And when he's done whatever shit job I find to give him, I'll take him to my house and I'll, like, make him clean out my recording

179

studio, the one I'm gonna have built, and while he's clean-
ing, he can get a good look at all my platinum records . . .

Satisfied, I sit down in the grass and wait for Austin
and the other guy to finish playing. And then I realize I'm
still holding my mom's shopping list with his name on it.
I'm about to throw it away and then I think, maybe I'll
keep it. Like, a couple million bucks could always come in
handy . . .

TWENTY-TWO

This is getting to be ridiculous! Feels like I've been out here a hundred years. Like all I've done all my life is struggle around this goddam court fighting heat and pain and exhaustion and thirst, and still the end's nowhere in sight.

Who is this Jack Winston anyway that I can't find a single weakness? Can't humble him, break him, stop him? There has to be a way. But what? And how much longer can I keep this up myself? Don't know. Just know that what I start, I finish. And that I've played too long, given too much, to quit now. But damn, this is punishment! All I'm doing is holding my own. Hanging on to my serve as though my life depended on it. And wondering all the while what that says about my priorities.

There's a muscle pulling deep in my thigh. Or maybe it's a cramp? Don't remember pulling it. Just know one minute I didn't know I had a thigh, next minute, I did. It's not serious. Nothing I can't compensate for, camouflage, play through. But it's one more thing to think about. Like the Jack Daniel's I drank last night. Don't know why that should be bothering me now. It's never done a thing for me one way or the other before except pass the time. Course, I haven't had to play tennis like this before either. Not in the last couple hundred years anyway.

The coffee I drank this morning isn't helping any either. Cups and cups of it to jolt me awake and get me going. It's here haunting me now with waves of bile and a shakiness that's blurring my vision and pounding my heart.

What the hell am I doing here anyway? This isn't what I had in mind when I invited him over. This whole damn match is getting to feel like the rest of my life. Something I started with good intentions and a desire to achieve, then watch turn sour, become a burden, something I'd like to walk away from. And the joke is, I know I brought it all on myself. Just like everything else.

Right now there's nothing I'd like better than to just leave. That or hurl my racquet in amongst these aimless, self-satisfied fools sitting around here waiting to see me toppled. I'd like to tell them to fuck off and leave us alone. To go do something useful with themselves for a change. Isn't a motherfucker among them hasn't sat across my desk or cornered me at parties, mouthing flatteries, while all the time I'm waiting, taking bets with myself, as to how and when they're going to hit me up for whatever it is they need. Do any of them know, understand, the price I've paid to put myself in a position where I can make all their piddling problems go away?

And who makes my problems go away? Who do I go bleed to? Who tells me what's happening to me lately and why I'm going off the tracks? Them? Huh! Jack? Why would I go burdening him when he's the only guy in this entire town who's never once come whining to me when I know there's been plenty of times in the past – and in the present from what I hear – when my bank and my name could pull him through a tight financial squeeze.

'Four-all,' Hal calls, and I think, Wonderful! Four games apiece, one set apiece. Hours of struggle and sweat and deuces coming out my ears, and what in hell have we accomplished? Nothing. Not a goddam thing.

I look over at Jack and see his face mottled a dull red, sweat guttering off every side of him, hear his breathing hard and labored like my own, and I know he's hurting as much as I am and I wonder what's his problem.

His teeth still show white between mustache and beard, but that's no smile he's wearing. That's a fighter's grimace. A guy, teeth bared, out to win. And I wonder, is this a gallant heart I'm watching or an obstinate fool? A guy, like myself, playing because he said he would? Because he's afraid he'd be thought less of a man if he quit? Hardly likely. Not with his track record.

Must be true then that the traits that irritate us most in others are the ones we're guilty of ourselves, because if this is a show of tenacity I'm watching, I don't like it. I'd respect him a whole lot more if he'd quit. Let go. Walk away from it. Say, without apology, 'This stopped being fun a long time ago and turned into a marathon and I don't need it. Catch you later.'

That's what I'd expect from a guy like him. What I wish I had the guts to say myself.

And he isn't going to do it – give me what I'm afraid to ask for myself – any more than Ellen is going to help me out and file for the divorce I crave with all my heart.

I asked her once, when she hadn't spoken to me in two weeks and the tension was more than I could stand, if she wouldn't be happier without me.

She'd thought about that awhile, her back to me, and while I waited for her reply I'd stared at the crystal prisms of the chandelier overhead, watching them stir and shimmer in the air conditioning blowing from a side vent, scarcely able to breathe over the hope growing in my heart.

The air clicked off at the same time Ellen turned, and as the prisms grew still, my hope died. She had adopted the pose, one of several in her repertoire, of a coy child. A pose I'd found appealing in times gone by when she had been young and childlike. A pose that's ugly now, unseemly, coming as it does from an overweight, middle-aged woman.

'How can you even think such a thing?' she'd lisped, shuffling forward with short hesitating steps, then standing before me, her shoulders moving back and forth like a child unable to keep itself still. 'I'm your baby, remember? The one who stood by you when you were a nobody and who worked so hard to get you where you are today. The one who waited all those years for you when I could have had any man in town . . . ' She'd paused to look up at me, letting me see her eyes fill with tears. 'And don't forget, I'm the one you promised to cherish. The one who almost died having your babies.'

'It's only that no matter what I do, what I give you, you remain so unhappy . . . ' I'd faltered, writhing with guilt, yet at the same time hating her for the ugly game she was playing, for the steel that glinted behind the tears. 'I thought perhaps' – and I'd taken her in my arms so she

184

couldn't read my face – 'you'd be so much happier without me.'

'What an old fool you are,' she'd said, stepping back, her pose forgotten, knowing she'd won and turning the knife. 'As if you could get along without me. Why, we grew up together. I'm your best friend. In fact, your only friend. Who else can you trust? Who knows you as I do? And who else, in spite of what you've become, still puts up with you? I do. And as trying as you are, as thoughtless and as wrapped up in yourself as you are, I'll never leave you. Never. Now, promise me you'll never talk like this again and then you can go fix that leaky faucet I was telling you about. You know, the one in the pool shower. Promise . . . ?'

What could I do? Cursing my cowardice, I promised. And now the best I can hope for is that she dies first . . .

A chill shudders through me at those last words. Here in this steaming heat I'm shaking and my movements feel stiff and jerky as the reality of what I'm thinking hits home. My ears are ringing as though someone who'd been talking to me in a soft, lulling monotone for years suddenly put their lips to my ear and shouted one obscene sentence, then pulled away, leaving me with the echo of the words repeating themselves over and over in my head, 'The best I can hope for is that she dies first.'

Jesus Christ! Is that what I really think? Is that what I'm doing? Plodding through my nights and my days hoping Ellen will have the decency to die first and let me off the hook, save me the embarrassment of admitting I failed? And what if she's not willing to do that? And is that what I'm doing here now with Jack? Waiting for him to quit so I can live up to my reputation – that of a man of his word, ready to die over a few points of a game – rather than face up to my own feelings? Why should he?

And why should I wait? What for? So I can congratulate myself at the end of it all? Prove to the world that I stuck it out, honored my commitments? Who will be impressed? Who will care? These people? Jack? What's it to them? They couldn't care less. Then what am I doing to myself?

I hear, as from far away, applause, people stamping their feet on the wooden steps of the stands, and I'm so confused I'm damned if I know what's going on. I don't know what the score is. Where we are in games . . .

'Five-four,' Hal calls, and I'm relieved. Five and four makes nine, and nine is an odd number, so that means we can go in for a break. And if that was my point, and it was obviously a game point, then that means that I held serve, and if I can figure all that out, then I'm not screwing up as badly as I think I am. Just a little confused.

Maybe the sun's gotten to me. Maybe I'm delirious and don't know it. I feel different, I tell you, as though hearing those monstrous words jolted me enough to shift focus and see myself and my life from a different angle.

From this new, unfamiliar viewpoint I see Ellen isn't my problem. Neither are my kids. Or Jack. Or anything else I've been pointing my finger at, though I could have gone to my grave thinking they were. My problem is me. The self-pitying fool who's been going around asking inanimate objects, 'What happened?' The one who'd rather wallow in despair, blaming others for his unhappiness, than take

186

responsibility for it himself and do something about it.

From this perspective I have no qualms divorcing Ellen. I don't hate her. Not anymore. What I hate is what we've been doing to each other. And I see that to stay is to destroy us both; that living a lie, holding myself up to be what I'm not – a loving, devoted husband, when all the time I'm wishing her dead – is a far uglier, more deceitful thing than going back on a vow given years ago when the world and I were not what we are today, and the thought that either could change never entered my mind.

I expect there'll be screaming. Tears. Expect she'll make me out a heartless monster to the kids and anyone else who cares to listen, but that's OK. She'll be right up to a point, anyway. I am a monster. A spineless monster who, had he really been thinking of others instead of himself, would indeed have left her years ago when she still had some youth and looks going for her. Sorry, Ellen. I thought I was doing us both a favor. I honestly did.

She'll want for nothing. She never has and she never will. That part of the bargain I can keep, and if that's guilt talking, then let it talk. I feel guilty as hell.

I'll do the same for the kids. See they never want. But more than that, I'll step aside and let them grow up. Let them find their own paths instead of trying to buy their lives for them, crippling them with my wealth.

Lord! Lord! Forgive me my trespasses. Not only for what I've done to others but for what I've made of myself: a pitiful, bitter old fart who'd rather play with himself than face up to his shortcomings. A stubborn fool with outworn ideas trying to fill commitments filled to overflowing years ago. Trying to keep us all locked into a mold we grew out of a long, long time ago.

'You ready?' Hal asks, leaning down to touch me on the shoulder.

'How about Jack?' I ask, opening my eyes. 'Is he ready?'

'Out there on the court, waiting . . .'

I look over and see Jack standing where I had stood in the last game and the ball boys tossing balls down his end. That means he's up for serve, and if the score is five-four, that also means I held serve that last game. How about that? And I didn't even know it . . .

I hesitate a moment, uncertain how a guy who's just done a three-hundred-and-sixty-degree turn on his life should handle a thing like this. I really don't want to go back out on that court again. I feel drained. Mentally and physically exhausted. Older and tireder than I've ever felt in all my forty-eight years. And I know if I thought I was fighting for this match earlier, it's going to seem like games in the park to what I'm going to have to come up with to bring this one home. And if I'm going to start living a new way, start doing what's right for me, then shouldn't I begin now?

I look over to where Jack's propping up the fence, waiting, and I think of the fight he's put up all morning. Of how his play forced me to face myself. And I think, I owe him. I catch myself snorting at that. Isn't that what I've been guilty of all my life? Hanging on when it's time to let go? Putting others ahead of myself? And isn't that what I just decided not to do anymore? I'm not sure. I haven't had time to work it out yet, but I think what I just decided to do was change course when I've made a mistake, not live with it.

Anyway, if going out there again is being a spineless wonder, then let me be a spineless wonder one more time. At least I can be a fighting one, and man, is he going to have to fight for this! I'm not that far gone on sunstroke, or mixed-up emotions or whatever else it is I've got, to let him walk away without showing him the best I'm capable of. And besides, I plain don't know how to play this game any other way.

I pull myself out of my chair, and none too soon. I can feel my stiffening muscles protest, particularly the one in my thigh. That one is going to need attention. Later . . .

'Yeah, Austin!' someone calls.

'Go get him,' says another.

'Make us proud!'

I acknowledge their goodwill with a wave of the hand, but I don't look back. I can't spare that much energy. But I'm glad they're there. I don't see them as heartless, conniving leeches out to use me anymore, but as decent, familiar friends come to see me through some kind of crisis I don't have a name for yet. And I feel like I owe them for sticking around. How come I'm still owing everybody? I don't owe anybody anything.

'One thing,' I call when I'm halfway across the court, stopping so my glance takes in everyone present. 'If we ever get to six-all, we play a tiebreaker, OK? I'm not screwing around in this heat any longer than I have to.' And I resume my march, pleased with what I just said. It seemed as nice a compromise as any I could make, given where I'm coming from and where I'm going to. And it did come from the gut!

TWENTY-THREE

'Give me a break!' I hear myself howl, and then I'm firing my racquet across the court to where, even though this is an even game, I intend to sit, and slowly, because it's harder now to walk a straight line than chase after a ball, I follow after it.

Je-sus! How much punishment does a man have to take? How long does he have to wait for that one short ball, one unforced error, one moment of inattention, before he can crack that armor, break that serve, and get the hell off this nightmare court?

Aren't there more important things to put yourself on the line for than this? This is supposed to be a game, for chrissakes. Fun! A couple hours sport, a few beers, a quiet talk with Austin, then home. Maybe in time for lunch. Lunch? Jesus, the way I'm going I'll be lucky to make it for dinner. Carried in on a stretcher . . . cold compresses on my pulses . . . IVs gurgling . . .

It's five-all and what have we got? Ten games! Gone already! History! And I'm no closer to beating him now than I was whenever the hell it was we started this mother-fucking match.

I turn my head to look over at Austin, and even that much effort hurts. The pull in my shoulder's moved up to grab at my neck as well, but I'm curious to know if it's just me taking this whole frigging match out of proportion, or is he too? And if he is, then why? What's in it for him? What's he trying to prove? Why can't he, for once in his life, give up on something before it's finished? I'd respect him more. I really would.

He's not looking too fresh now, I tell you, sitting there limp, head drooping, face streaming, that pretty pink shirt of his stained dark.

I want to look behind me, see if we've still got an audience, but I'm not going to do it. Not going to risk any more pain than I already have. And I really don't care. If they're there, they're quiet. Haven't heard a sound out of them. Or maybe it's me, not listening. Maybe they've been cheering themselves hoarse. I wouldn't know. All I hear out there is the sound of my own breathing, the blood roaring in my ears, my feet pounding, sliding, scratching across the dried-up clay. That and Hal's voice calling score. A voice of doom when it's Austin's point. The archangel Gabriel's when it's mine.

I hear Austin's feet scraping, the squeal of his chair as his body leaves it, and then he's straightening, stretching, reaching for his racquet. He smiles up at Hal, says something that makes them both laugh, and then he's looking my way, his eyes asking am I ready? I nod and he winks and strides off, his gaze distant, not looking tired anymore, but purposeful. Like Douglas MacArthur returning to the Philippines . . .

I stare after him and for a moment, a terrible moment that

lasts too long and nails me to my chair, I choke. For all my talk of what I can do and what I'm going to do and blah, blah, blah . . . seeing Austin walk away like that, so strong still, so . . . so damn confident, puts doubt in my mind.

I plain don't know if I've got enough gas left to wade through much more of this. Not and come up with the kind of play I'm going to need to crack him before he cracks me, I don't. And I don't know if this shoulder, this neck, can hold up for maybe two more service games. Maybe I've left it too late. Frittered away my reserves on moments of dazzle in the early sets. Maybe I've screwed up royally.

My mouth runs dry thinking of the possibility of leaving here a loser when all along I've been counting on this match, Austin, as my ticket to a fresh start. Is that what I've done – now and all my life? Counted on tomorrow, the next shot, the next joke, to bail me out of the mistakes of the past? And have I counted once too often?

I feel the blood drain out of my face, the sweat on my body grow clammy cold, and I think, Jesus, is this the end of the line? Does there come a day when you reach inside yourself for more and nothing's there? When you can't get up and go on? When you hear yourself say, 'I can't'? And is this going to be the day? Is this how it feels to grow old?

I see ahead of time and it's evening. This evening. And Austin's mixing drinks at his poolside bar. Long green shadows filter the setting sun and there's an occasional drift of smoke from the barbecue. He's surrounded by people, all of them dressed like he is – like they're posing for a cruise ship ad – all of them laughing up the story he's telling. The story of the three-setter he won this morning.

There are nods of understanding, murmurs of appreciation, as he acts out some of the finer points. And he's shaking his own head at the wonder of it. Telling about the deuces, the heat, the crowd . . .

He's telling them about me, too. A guy he went to school with – high school, you understand, not college – and he's saying, 'He's an OK kind of a guy. A bit loud. A bit crude, maybe. But fun to be around. You know, once in a while when you want a real workout.'

Will he tell them I hit him up for a loan? Will he? No. Austin's not like that. Austin's ethical. A man of his word. Anyway, face it. I don't win this match, I'm not asking for a loan. I'm not leaving here a loser and a beggar both . . .

The old fears, the familiar ones, the ones I keep locked and bolted away, come crowding through the door opened by my imagination and fight for attention. In swift succession I see myself reading Jennie's farewell note. 'Sorry, darling, I really am. But . . . ' And she'll go on to give me a hundred reasons, valid reasons, why she has to go and why she can't stay, and then she'll finish it off nice and friendly and say something like ' . . . and stay in touch, hear! Call me once in a while and let me know how you are.'

I hear the phone ringing and it's the deals I've got going now, the ones I'm counting on to put food on the table. 'Sorry, old guy,' the voices come smarming out of the receiver, 'BUT . . . we just found ourselves a deal we can't pass up. Yeah. Sixty-five feet. Sleeps ten. Mint condition. Radar. You and the missus'll have to come take a ride sometime. Give us your seal of approval . . . '

I see my car on the back of a wrecker. My car! How can a man live without his car?

I taste bile in my mouth and it's ugly. Bitter. Like failure. I spit it out and sorry if that offends you, ma'am . . .

Somehow I get my feet under me, grope around for my racquet, see it upended where I tossed it earlier. I hoist myself out of the chair, stumble towards it, and I know I better do something, think something, and I better do it quick.

Remembering an old trick I taught myself when I was a green kid wanting to make a living selling, and too clammy scared to pick up a phone, knock on a door, I imagine I see myself up on a movie screen. And what I see is this poor, pitiful schmuck bent double with fear, stumbling around playing for time.

What are you? I sneer at it, my eyes narrow, my lips tight with scorn, a man or a creep? You get to choose. Get to see yourself any way you want, so what'll it be? Want to see yourself young or old? Proud or humbled? Stooped or tall? Winning or losing? What'll it be, jerk? Tell me. Want to laugh or cry? Want to see Austin serving victory cocktails over your dead body tonight or yourself coming through the door a winner, telling Jennie, 'I did it! I beat the sucker and I got the loan. He's bailing us out!'

I take a deep breath while I'm coming upright, racquet in hand, and I hold it. I've made my choices and I'm looking long and hard at the last frame, savoring its every detail.

And then I let it all go. The picture and my breath both. And I'm sauntering out on the court like I don't have a care in the world. My gut's sucked in, my back's straight,

194

and I'm damned if this is going to be the day I say my first 'I can't.'

The kid tosses me a ball. I catch it on my racquet, give it a couple of bounces, and then toss it up and swing at it. And though pain sears through my shoulder and shoots up my neck, I lean into the serve, follow it to net, volley Austin's return, back up for an overhead, and letting the pain flow like it's part of the game, slam it into a corner where he can't get to it. And while I'm walking back to the baseline I'm thinking, That's how it's gonna be, folks. From here on out. No more razzle-dazzle. No more trick shots between the legs or around the net posts. From now on, what you see is what you get. Me playing like a grown man. Me knowing I'm going to win and doing whatever I have to do till you and Austin know it too.

TWENTY-FOUR

I'm doing OK while the points are in play. That's the easy part. Then I'm absorbed enough just getting to the ball, getting it back over the net, that I forget myself. But oh, God . . . in between . . . walking back to the baseline . . . Regrouping on a court that's swaying . . . pitching . . . That's the hard part. That's when I become aware of the high-pitched ringing in my ears, the taste of salt in my mouth, the weakness in my legs . . .

I keep telling myself to knock it off. To stop playing the hero. To quit before I fold and make a total ass of myself. But then I see the ball coming at me again and I think, What the hell? What's one more? And like I said, while I'm going for it I forget the rest and I'm hitting it back thinking, This has to be the last point. It has to be. And then I see Jack hitting it back again and I think, I guess it wasn't . . .

I've lost track of the score. Can't hear what Hal's calling over my body's distress and I'm past caring. All I want now, my sole aim, is to finish this thing upright.

And now what's going on? Why is Jack howling like that? Hal coming down out of his chair? Unless . . . My God, can it be? Is it . . . ? Is it over? It is! Must be! Else why are all these people on the court, surging around us, thumping our backs, shaking our hands, saying, 'Holy cow, you guys! Where'd you ever learn to play like that?' And,

'You sure you two haven't been lying about your age?' And,

'Man, I'd have known I was going to be watching world-class tennis, I'd have put it on film, made a video . . . '

And now they're pushing us into chairs, handing us drinks, soaking towels in ice water and slapping them on our heads, the backs of our necks. And I'm laughing, talking along with the rest of them – or my reflexes are – I have no idea what I'm saying. All I'm aware of is relief. Such sweet blessed relief it's over and I'm still conscious, I can't tell you . . .

TWENTY-FIVE

The end's coming fast now, it's coming. One minute we're at thirty-all, my serve, five-six in games, the next I'm staring wild-eyed at the opening I've been waiting for, praying for, all these long, murderous hours: a lob, nudged by a gust of wind from an approaching storm, floating down short in my service area. I see Austin backing up, ready to field the overhead he expects from me, and to keep him there, though I dread the pain, I wind up for one. But at the last possible moment, a moment that feels like eternity, I drop my racquet, step back, let the ball bounce, and, almost shaking with concentration, slice that mother for a drop shot that needs such timing, I swear I stop breathing watching it skim back across the net with only its fuzz to spare. And even while I'm watching it, seeing it lazily revolving as though in slow motion, I hear the thud of Austin's feet coming in and I marvel that after all he's been through, he still has enough left to even try for it. And still that ball is on its way down, hasn't landed, and he's getting closer and I'm yelling, 'Die, dammit . . . die!'

And whether I'm saying it out loud or to myself, I don't know. All I know is, it's all I can do not to reach over the net and slap it down, finish its journey for it. But then it lands, kicks back on itself away from Austin's outstretched racquet, and I leave the ground myself in a wild explosion of joy.

Yes, there's another point to play through to hold serve. And a tiebreaker after that to fight for, and I have to sit on myself hard to forget that one shot and go on to the others. But it gave me the confidence I needed, the drive, something to feed on so that every shot after it surpasses the one before and I become exhilarated, painless, high on myself thinking, Go on, baby! Go for it! Give it everything you've got! Let it happen . . .

And while I'm hammering home these last points I'm out of myself, marveling at what I'm still capable of doing. Thinking, Look at you! Moments ago you didn't think you had it in you to get out of a chair! Didn't think you had anything left to give. And all the time there was still this much left inside, untapped, waiting . . .

And so I played on in a kind of ecstasy of self-belief thinking, Where've you been these last few hours – these last years – man? You came here scared. At the end of your rope. Ready to crawl. Beg. Ready to throw in the towel. Willing to do anything at all but grow up and move on. Can you believe that? That you were willing to live like a coward, clinging to the security of this nothing little town like a barnacle sucked up to a seawall? Using your friends, your connections, your kids, anything you could think of, so you wouldn't have to let go and start over.

And look at you now! You don't look like a beggar to me now! Not anymore, you don't. Not the kind of guy I'd expect to see tippy-toeing around an old friend sniffing out a loan. Jesus! Looking at you now, seeing you so strong still, in the prime of your life, I'd take you for the kind who'd have sense enough to walk away from something that was used up – wrung dry – years ago and start over someplace else where the opportunities match the talent. Someone who'd be giving a lot of thought to those offers that keep coming in from the East Coast and everyplace else where there's open water and big, beautiful boats. And man, that's not running, that's facing facts.

And with each stroke, each thought, I feel bigger, stronger, until I'm thinking, Let 'em take the frigging car! Damn thing's falling apart under the hood anyway. Plenty more where it came from, aren't there? Here or in Germany. I mean, why not try dignified next time around and get me a car like Austin's?

Next thing I know I hear Hal's voice calling, 'Game, set, and match . . . ' And I'm leaving the court in a daze, sorry to hear it's over when I still had so much more to give.

TWENTY-SIX

The crowd is thinning now, trickling away the way they came, in twos and threes, everyone going back to their own games, their own lives, and I'm glad. I felt strangely uncomfortable around them, like I was a fraud. I couldn't bring myself to look them in the eyes knowing they are still taking me for the old Austin, the happily married paragon of virtue, when I know that Austin died out there somewhere in the last set. And maybe they won't like the guy that's coming. The one that up and left his wife and kids after all those years and started acting crazy. They'll say I'm acting crazy whether I act crazy or not. Ever hear of a divorce where the one doing the divorcing isn't labeled crazy? Crazy or worse . . .

'You sure there's nothing more we can get for you guys?' I hear the departing voices call to our inert forms. 'Another drink? A sandwich, maybe? Some ice?'

'No,' we say, one or the other, to each question. 'Nothing, thanks. Just need some rest. Not hungry right now . . . '

'Later, maybe? We'll be glad to come back later.'

'Yeah. Later. Much later. Like when we can walk and get it ourselves. But thanks . . . '

'Yeah. Thanks anyway.'

And then the last voice dies away, the last footstep, and we're alone, Jack and I, the way we were years ago when it all began, and here's a funny thing: Although I've spent the last few hours – hours that seem like days – following Jack's every movement, every expression, with the closeness of a hawk circling for the kill, what I'm seeing now behind my closed lids is the kid he used to be. And I see myself, a tall, lanky boy walking out to the court in the old neighborhood thinking myself unobserved.

A long time I'd been waiting, watching from behind my bedroom curtains for the last, late afternoon stragglers to leave the park so I could go practice what burned in my head. And finally, enticed by the smell of cooking food floating out of open windows, the park emptied and the court was mine.

I didn't see Jack sitting cross-legged in the deep shadow of the backboard until I was nearly on top of him and then it was too late. My face burned red and my eyes watered, knowing he had to have been there all along, watching me, and I hated him for it. And I didn't know what to do about it. Turn around and leave or ask him to please move so I could use the board? Even though I didn't want to use the board with him there.

He didn't help me out. Didn't say a word. Just sat there grinning that fool grin of his. And I stood there feeling bigger and clumsier with every passing second . . .

Finally, 'I've been waiting on you,' he said.

'Yeah?' I said. 'What for?'

His smile widened and he got to his feet and came

towards me. 'So I can beat the shit out of you,' he said with that characteristic charm of his. 'Why else?'

That must have been the first time we ever played, one of the first anyway, and it only seems like yesterday. And now look at us. Two old guys with aging, exhausted bodies too tired to move, too tired to talk. And where the years between went, how we ever got from there to here, don't ask me.

What I feel right now is that I'm on the last leg of a journey. A journey that went on way too long. I feel the way I feel when I've been strapped in a plane seat so long I'm numb, and even though a voice on a loudspeaker has told me we're cleared to land, I still have to sit, helpless, through the interminable ear-aching descent, the thud of the landing gear falling into place, the reversing of the jets, the jar of the wheels hitting the runway, and still it's forever before I'm free to get up and start moving around on my own again.

My heartbeat is nearly back to normal. So is my breathing. And if I open my eyes, things I look at are stationary again and not wavering as though I'm looking at them through deep water. But I still feel like I died out there and the new me, if there is one, has yet to draw his first breath.

He will. In time he will. I don't expect to keep the world on hold much longer. And while I wait for the right moment to come, it's not unpleasant lounging here in a kind of limbo, not having to be either what I was or what I hope to become.

Maintenance is here now, working on the court we just played on. All of them busy with rollers and brooms and tape brushes. The sprinklers will go on next, long arms of water laying the dust of the storm we churned up. And in a few minutes every trace of our match will be smoothed away, the court looking as fresh and unblemished as the day it was laid out. And that hardly seems right. Seems like there ought to be something left out there to show what we put ourselves through today. But what do I want? Bronze busts, one of each of us, staring forever sightless at the mess we made? Come on!

I chuckle, start to turn to Jack, and come up short, every muscle, every atom of my being screaming in protest. Jesus! There isn't an inch of me that doesn't feel like it's been hit more than once by a Mack truck. And I always prided myself on being in shape.

Stiff as a board then, I push myself upright, try stretching, give it up as hopeless, and walking the way I am, like an ancient crab, shuffle over to where Jack's lying flat on his back on a redwood bench. Very carefully, as though it's something I've never done before and need to learn how, I lower myself into a chair beside him.

'Boy, but we showed them, though, didn't we?' I say, after I've got myself as comfortable as I'm going to get.

He grunts, wiggles his fingers, letting me know he's listening.

'Who'd of ever thought,' I go on after another long rest, 'back when we lived in the old neighborhood, there'd come a day when at this age – this ancient age, mind you – we'd put on the show we were saving for Wimbledon, huh? Centre Court . . . '

He opens one eye, smiles, lets it close.

'Hey, come on,' I say. 'You can do better than that. Show a little interest . . . '

'Interest?' he moans. 'Man, you nearly killed me out there and now you want interest?'

'It wasn't that bad, was it?'

'No. No, it wasn't. It was worse.'

'Yeah? You mean you were hurting too? I thought it was just me. Thought you were still just warming up. Wish I'd known. I'd have really made it tough. Well, if it's any consolation, you didn't exactly make it easy on me either.'

'I didn't? You could have fooled me. But that's good. That's very good. I'm glad to hear it.'

I lie back in my chair and let my eyes close. There's a storm not far off. The kind we get here afternoons this time of year. Big indigo clouds rolling in off the bay. Thunder crashing. Lightning spewing. Then torrents of rain followed by blue skies and steaming earth. Meantime, the breeze ushering it in feels good.

I stir, check to see Jack's still there, then start saying what's going through my mind. 'Do you suppose,' I muse, 'we could have done it better? I mean, if we'd played this match a long time ago, say right after I came home from school and you were Mr Hotshot. Do you suppose we could have played it any better than we did today?'

His eyes stay shut, but the skin around them crinkles, and I know he's laughing. 'No,' he says. Then again, 'No.'

He's right. The answer is no. Back then in our youth with muscles like strong new elastic, blood clean and unpolluted, minds keen and free of the strivings and treacheries of the years between, we were raw still, untried. Back then, though our ambition burned fierce, we thought life was forever.

205

Thought if we didn't win today, we would tomorrow. Thought it was just a matter of time.

Time! The word makes me wince with fresh pain. How much do I have left? Enough to tear apart what I've spent a lifetime creating and put it back together in a different pattern? What if I can't do it? Jesus Christ, I'm forty-eight already. Nearly forty-nine. In another year I'll be fifty. A whole half century gone already. Used up. And in all those years I came no closer to being comfortable, at peace with myself, than I was back in high school. And I think, you're going to start over now? Where will you begin? And suppose what you put together this time around is as fucked up as the last?

I let out a groan I hope Jack takes for physical protest, and wonder how long a man has to live before all the pieces come together.

I turn to Jack, clear my throat. I'm ready at last to ask the questions I've wanted answered all my life. Ready to open myself up to anything and everything he can tell me. And . . . I don't voice a single one of them. Seeing him lying the way he is, like a corpse, his eyes closed, unchallenging, answers them all.

He may have wrung me dry today, pushed me further than I thought I could go, but I know I'm fooling myself thinking he's led a charmed life. He's had it as rough as me, maybe rougher, and it's showing. I see it in the fat bulging over the sides of the bench, in the gray streaking the hair of his face and head, in the deep lines around his eyes and mouth. But I see, too, a guy with a lot of living left to do, a lot of growing, and in a while, in his noisy, wacky way, he'll get up and go do it. Try, anyway. And if the day never comes when I get all my pieces to fit, neither will he. And I think maybe that's good because I have a feeling, a suspicion, that when the pieces do fit, it's over.

I look around me and see that everything's the same as it's always been. Nothing's changed. But I recognize that nothing will ever be the same again either because I've changed. I'm no more the guy that walked out here a few hours ago – a century ago – than I'm head of Citicorp. That guy would never have taken a beating on his own turf and sat around afterwards feeling good about himself. That's got to mean something. Course, maybe all it means is that I'm having a delayed reaction. That I'll be climbing the walls tomorrow, putting myself through all the usual shit I put myself through when I haven't lived up to my expectations. Calling Hal for private lessons. Getting up early to work on the backboard – early so no one sees me. But then again, maybe I won't care any more tomorrow than I do today. And another odd thing. I'm not sitting here asking what happened, am I? I know what happened. I lost. And I know that doesn't make me less a man or Jack more a man. It just makes me a man who lost a game of tennis. Period.

Sure, winning is better. It's what you play for. But for me, today, knowing who I played, what I played through, knowing I lasted, seems to be enough. And I can let it go. Like I did my marriage, knowing some things are just too hard. Even for me.

TWENTY-SEVEN

A long, drowsy while I've been lying here, thinking every minute I'll get up the next, and not doing a thing about it. What I should've done, coming off the court, was keep going while I still had it in me. Just gotten in my car and taken off. Now I think I'm too tired to ever move again. Like I'm not so much lying here as splatted here, a mindless blob with no will to ever move again.

My head is filled, crammed, with half-finished thoughts, slow-moving images. As though I had a video camera out there with me and now I'm taking the time to look at the results.

There's a lot of good tennis there to see. Some so spectacular I run it by slow so I can see for myself, remind myself, how it was and who did what to who. Course, I keep going back, again and again, to that drop shot. That motherfucking drop shot . . .

I've got lots of footage on Austin. Miles of it. As though he's permanently imprinted on the backside of my eyes. Like when I've been out on a boat all day and come night, when I close my eyes to sleep, all I see is vast heaving seas and a vaster sky.

Studying Austin on my film, watching him serve, cover the court, pace the baseline, stay so goddamned, ruthlessly tough from first to last, I'm thinking, Man, he's something else, that Austin Sinclair! He pushed me to the edge of despair today. Forced me to look long and hard at what it is I am, and what it is to be a man who refuses to give up. And yet for all that, I see that he wasn't the enemy. He was only the catalyst. The enemy was that smothering burden of fear I took out there with me. And that's what Austin forced me to overcome. And man, it was so colossal, I'm surprised it doesn't show up there alongside the rest of the stuff I'm looking at. Then I think, How could that be, jerk? Since when does fear stand around and pose for photographs?

After a long while of mulling over all that's passed, my mind wanders off to what's to come – to pictures not yet taken – and I see myself opening the door to our apartment, Jennie looking up, her face expectant.

'I did it!' I hear myself crowing. 'I beat the sucker!' And she's coming towards me laughing.

'What did I tell you?' she says. 'Didn't I tell you?'

But maybe I won't do it like that. Maybe I'll go in dragging, my head down so she can't read my face, acting like I lost, then surprise her. Like hell I will! I can't do that. That's all she's looked at since the day I married her, me coming through the door like a whipped dog.

What I'll do is, I'll go in with flowers behind my back. Roses. I'll charge them. With any luck we'll be gone before the statement comes due.

'Sweet thing,' I'll say. 'If you could have your heart's

desire. Anything in this whole wide wonderful world, what would it be?'

Of course, she'll say she's already got it – me – and I'll kiss her for that and repeat the question. She'll look at me puzzled, trying to figure out what it is I want her to say, and she'll try again. Maybe she'll get it next time around and maybe she won't. But sooner or later she'll say something like, 'What I'd really like, more than anything, is to go off someplace with you. Someplace new where nobody knows us and we can start over, just the two of us . . . ' Like she's said so many, many times before. And that's when she'll get the roses.

Thinking along those lines, I'm ready to get up and leave, and in another little while, I will. I will . . . Just want to savor a moment longer what happened here today and then I'll gather myself up for what's to come. It's nice here. Peaceful. Nobody left but Austin and me. Two old guys too pooped to pop.

I hear him shuffling around and I know he's parked himself in a chair beside me, though I don't open my eyes to see. He starts talking about the match, chuckling to himself, and I wonder if those friends of his – the ones watching earlier – have any idea what a truly great guy this is under the austere front he puts on. If they suspect what he's put himself through to become what he is.

Hardly likely. They don't know where he came from like I do. Or if they ever did, they forgot and believed the myths instead. Most likely they think he had the money and the connections from the first and all he had to do was show up and collect the prize. That if they'd just had his luck, they'd

210

be sitting where he is now, king of the hill. And they're wrong. All of them. Austin is what he is, head and shoulders above the rest of us, because he took everything that ever came his way – and there wasn't a whole hell of a lot – and ran with it. And while he was running, he never missed a beat, never fumbled the ball, never slacked off, and never, ever, gave up on the idea of himself.

I rate Austin up there with my dad, my sons. And there's no place higher you can go in my book.

TWENTY-EIGHT

'Come on,' I say, leaning over to grab Jack's knee and shaking it. 'I'll buy you a beer.'

He comes upright slowly, whimpering all the way. 'Can't,' he says, rubbing at his neck. 'I gotta go.'

'Go? Where do you have to go?'

'Home. Told Jennie I'd try and make it for lunch.'

'You missed lunch, pal,' I tell him. 'That gives you a while till dinner. Call her. Tell her we ran over. Hey! You can't just up and leave. Not now. We've got a lot of catching up to do.'

He shakes his head. 'I know it,' he says. 'And we will. But not today, OK? I really do have to run.'

'Well . . . ' I say, surprised he doesn't want to go inside, glory in his win, be the center of attention. 'You know best what you have to do. Come on, I'll walk you to your car. Say . . . we've got some people coming in tonight. Nothing formal. Just a few people from the bank coming over for a barbecue. Why don't you and Jennie join us?'

And while the words are coming out of my mouth, I'm seeing Ellen's face when I tell her there's going to be two extra. I actually shudder thinking how she'll look when I tell her who they are.

He takes a long time answering. As long, in fact, as it takes us to walk to his car. And along the way I'm wondering if he heard what I said, the storm being as close as it is and thunder rolling to beat the band. But as he opens his car door, eases himself inside, he says, 'God, Austin . . . any other time and we'd have been tickled to death. But tonight . . . tonight we just can't make it. We've got plans from way back and we just can't break them.'

I want to tell him there isn't going to be another time. Not for a while anyway. And not under that roof. But I don't. That particular scene hasn't been played yet, and he'll hear about it soon enough. And to be honest, I'm relieved. A big scene with Ellen, I don't need. Not with the one that's coming.

I watch him settle himself in his car. He turns the key in the ignition and we've got instant, deafening music. He makes no move to turn it down, and I see by the preoccupation on his face he's not only going to leave, he already has. That his mind's gone on ahead to whatever else is next on his agenda. And I'm not ready to see him go. As though I'm afraid he'll take all my fragile new convictions with him and I'll be left with nothing.

'Hey!' I yell, pounding on the hood of his car to make him stop, keep him there. 'Hold on . . . I want to tell you . . . '

Frowning, he turns the volume down, and in the silence I'm staring down into those unreadable eyes of his with a head full of scrambled thoughts that won't line up into any sort of sense.

If I could shape them into sentences, they'd be about the admiration I've always had for him, and the respect, however grudging and tinged with envy it was. And I'd let him know that, just knowing he was around, even though I rarely saw him, always added spice to my achievements. And I'd tell him how I've missed being around him all these years and how I hope, once I'm through with what I have to go through, he'll be part of my life again. Like in the old days.

And if I could articulate, I'd want to thank him. I owe him a lot of thanks. What I'd thank him for the most would be just for being what he is and never pretending to be otherwise and for the way that honesty came through in his play today, showing me, by comparison, the dishonesty in myself.

But I don't know if he'd understand any of it. Can't be sure he wouldn't laugh at my words. Words I might regret tomorrow. And in the meantime the silence is growing. To cover it I reach out and grab his shoulder, give it a shake. 'I just wanted to tell you,' I say with a shrug, 'how good it was seeing you, playing you, again.'

He reaches up and grasps my hand. 'You too, old guy,' he says. 'You too.'

'We'll do it again sometime? Sometime soon?'

He laughs. 'Not too soon,' he says.

I take my hand away. 'You will stay in touch?' I say, because I don't want to force myself on him. Want to know it comes from him too.

'You bet,' he says. 'I'll call you at that fancy bank of yours.'

'Do that. Make sure they put you through too. Don't let them tell you I'm busy . . . In a meeting.'

'You've got a lot to learn about me, boy,' he says, 'if you think there's a switchboard I can't get past.'

And then the volume's back up on the radio, his foot's down on the accelerator, there's a wave of the hand, and he's gone.

Drops of rain big as quarters start slopping down on me and I'm diving for my car cussing him out because it's his fault it's parked where it is . . . that the sun roof's open.

I get the roof closed, dry off the seats, and then, like a convalescent who's overdone his first day out of bed, sit exhausted watching the rain batter the windshield on the outside, steam fog its way up the inside, and I know I can't go through with it.

What? Leave Ellen? I must be crazy. How can I? She's been part of my life since I was seventeen. We grew up together. Desert my kids? *My kids?* Leave my home? It's monstrous. Preposterous. Where would I go? Who would I be?

I'm sweating. Suffocating. Feeling as though I'm about to have cardiac arrest just thinking about it, and I fumble buttons and knobs to crack a window. Cool air and rain splatter in, but that's all the relief I get.

To get a grip on myself, make order out of chaos, I breathe deep and make myself go limp. Then, 'Think of your life the way it is,' I say reasonably, as though I'm talking to someone else. 'It's not really that bad, is it? Hell, you've lived it this many years, you can live it a few more.

Why rock the boat? Why run amok this late in life when this might just be a stage you're going through? A midlife crisis. You've got the bank. This club. Your tennis. And who knows but maybe one day she'll come to you asking for a divorce. Or surprise you and run away with the mailman . . . '

Thinking that, I know I'm only one short step away again from hoping she'll die first and I turn the key in the ignition and back out.

Ellen and I living silent and bitter year after year, both of us feeling trapped, resentful, each blaming the other, is that bad. It's very bad indeed. The story is over and one of us has got to turn the page.

I'll do it. I don't have a choice. Not everything in one day but one thing at a time, the way I play a game of tennis, one point at a time, then on to the next.

For today, it's enough that the decision's been made. I won't even mention it when I get home, not with people – my friends – coming in. She won't be speaking to me anyway. Won't say a word from the time I get home to the time the guests arrive, and then every other sentence out of her mouth will begin, 'Austin and I . . . ' and 'Austin always says, and I agree . . . ' Putting words into my mouth I wouldn't say under torture.

Tomorrow, call a hotel, one out on the beaches where I can get lost amongst the tourists for a while, and move out. I'll find the words when the time comes, and if I don't, well . . . my actions will speak for themselves.

Monday, call my attorney. Tell him to go ahead and do whatever it is attorneys do with the papers I drew up two years ago, then reneged on.

And so on. A day at a time, a ball at a time, until there are no more points to be played. Nothing left to do but walk out to a clean-swept court and start over.

TWENTY-NINE

'Come on,' Austin says. 'I'll buy you a beer.'

I'd like for him to buy me a beer. I'd like to buy him one too. Only . . . not right now. I'd have a beer with him right now, get to talking about old times, I might go soft on myself. Sentimental. Start trying to put into words the respect I've always had for him, the pride seeing his name up there in the headlines – even though there's always been a lot of jealousy there too – jealousy I hid behind sarcasm and laughter. And sitting there beside him at the bar, I might try to thank him for the way he played today, pushing himself to the limit when he didn't have a thing in the world to gain from it himself. And because just being around him again brought me to my senses. Set me straight. Ready to grow up and move on.

And I know I can't handle it. Get the words to come out right, I mean. Not knowing I won't be seeing him again, I can't. So all he'd have to drink with would be a guy muttering half-finished sentences into his beer, mush that would embarrass the both of us when what he wanted from me was a good time and a few laughs.

So I tell him some other time and gather up my stuff and

then, walking to the car, he says the one thing that comes close to undoing me. The thing I've been waiting to hear him say since I was eight years old. He says, 'We've got some people coming in tonight. Why don't you and Jennie join us?'

For a second, a moment no longer than a heartbeat, I let go of all my newfound resolutions and think, I don't have to leave! Not now! Why would I? I'm in like Flynn with him now! Back up beside him where I've always wanted to be and I can stay here. Play him weekends. Meet people. Get back on my feet. Why be hasty? Rush off like a fool chasing rainbows when everything I ever wanted is right here? And, my thoughts race on, if I pass up this chance, who knows but I won't be kicking myself around the block tomorrow? Beating my head against the wall for turning down what I came here to win? And what if this is just a weak moment I'm going through? What if all these grandiose schemes are just a hoax I'm pulling on myself because I had a great win? What then?

I'm tempted. So tempted I all but turn on the spot and ask him for the loan I came for, knowing that on a handshake it's mine.

But the feel of those last games is still strong inside me. The feel of my own power. And that's how I want to go on living. Not as a helpless victim of circumstances but as a creator of my own. In control. Playing it my way. And I know the potential for it in this town is all used up. That I'm cramped here. Stifled. And to stay is to bury myself alive.

So I tell him we have plans, Jennie and me. Lying because the whole leaving scene is so new to me, I can hardly grasp it myself and I need time to come to terms with it. And because while he's chatting on about times to come, I know there aren't going to be any times to come. Not for a long while anyway.

We're walking out to the parking lot while all this is going on, and rounding the bend, I see my car, safe where I left it and . . . I don't know . . . maybe it's because I'm so damn tired, I feel out of touch with reality. Or maybe it's knowing Austin is the first of the roots I'm going to have to pull up, and even this early on, I can tell that roots that go forty-eight years deep are not going to come up easy . . . Whatever . . . All I know is I'm hurting something fierce inside and I need to get out of here fast and that car looks like home to me. An oasis where I can hole up for a while. Get things straightened out. But will he let me go? No, he will not.

Austin has something to say, and either I'm going to let him say it or I'm going to have to run him down. So I sit there listening, only he doesn't say a thing. I look up when his hand comes down on my shoulder, but the light's wrong again and I can't read his face. Then he starts talking and all he says is, 'Nice seeing you again.' And for that he risks his life!

He says something else, I don't know what. Yes, I do. It's something about a rematch. And I hear myself say something back. Something trivial because I feel bogus sitting here talking about rematches when I know I'm leaving. And then I can't take it anymore, can't even take the time to close up my roof against the rain, and I turn the radio up loud, not to upset him but so I won't have to say good-bye. And I take off.

I'm about out of the lot before I take one last look in the rearview, and what I see is old Austin running to get out of the rain that is soaking us both. I can't see him too good what with the rain being so heavy and my eyes being all misted up, but what I see is comforting. I see Austin behaving exactly the way I'd expect Austin to behave caught short in a violent storm. I see him running like he's out for his own pleasure and the rain isn't falling on him at all.

He has a limp I hadn't noticed before, but otherwise he's carrying himself as tall and as dignified as ever and he has his hat on nice and straight.

'Old fart,' I say by way of farewell. And I mean it very kindly indeed.

Games Played

It hasn't quite happened
according to plan,
seems I've lost my way
since becoming a man.

It must have been fate
or the luck of the draw,
It's hard to imagine
how else I could fall.

Or perhaps, could it be,
the games that I played,
fooled hardly a soul
but the boy they betrayed?

Mike Dooley